DOCTOR WHO

THE COMPLETELY UNOFFICIAL ENCYCLOPEDIA

W9-AHF-754

mad
norwegian
press

CHRIS HOWARTH & STEVE LYONS

Copyright © 2006 Mad Norwegian Press,
www.madnorwegian.com
Cover art & interior design by Christa Dickson.

ISBN: 0-9725959-8-8
Printed in Illinois. First Edition: November 2006.

In memory of Moose (1991-2006) – a comedy legend.

ABOUT THIS BOOK

Well, here we are again. Has it only been ten years since the first *Completely Useless Encyclopedia*? How much has changed in that short decade! Virgin Publishing's *Doctor Who* imprint went etheric-beam-locators-up, and the BBC's EDAs and PDAs have come and gone, but now we have NSAs, BFs and other acronyms. The *Doctor Who Annual* is back – though one per year would have been enough for our bookshelves. In fact, there's more tie-in tat to collect than ever, from cufflinks to expandable flannels to talking Dalek bins; we've even got the Top Trumps set, sticker album and Corgi car we all wanted thirty years ago. As fans, we've had to learn exciting new words like Tardisode, webcast, VidFIRE, e-book and gay agenda. Beep the Meep has returned twice, and there are now three ongoing *Doctor Who* comic strips – while old TV episodes are available on space age silver discs. And what a treat to see both 'The Lion' and 'Day of Armageddon' returned to the archives.

We also recently heard that *Doctor Who* was back on the telly, on BBC Wales or something. Blimey, they'll be remaking *Battlestar Galactica* next!

Of course, we really wanted to write a follow-up to *The Completely Useless Star Trek Encyclopedia* (1997). Not just because Trekkies are so easy to wind up (see, we did it again there, by calling them Trekkies); no, we felt we needed to correct our assertion that there would be no reason to watch *Voyager* once Seven of Nine replaced Kes. How could we have been so wrong? So apologies to Jeri Ryan and her costume designer, though we were right about everything else in *Voyager* still being rubbish (we just did it again, look).

Anyway, we'd got about as far as noting that the CGI Gorn in *Enterprise* was less realistic than the one in *The Animated Series* when, out of the blue, Mad Norwegian publisher Lars Pearson asked for another *Doctor Who* volume instead. Apparently, the Welsh revival had found a resonance with the cultural zeitgeist – and it was quite popular too, which was a bonus. It was the prospect of cashing in on this popularity, coupled with the fact that the series now has cartoon CGI monsters of its own to mock, that made us say yes.

You may have noticed that, this time around, we're a *Completely Unofficial Encyclopedia*. Now, back in 1996, we did do a certain amount of pointing and laughing at fans who produced unlicensed tie-ins – but we have an excellent reason for here following in their footsteps. We were offered some money to do it. We did briefly hope to emulate those many other ex-official, ex-Virgin *Doctor Who* books out there, and just pad out our first effort with a few new entries – until, sadly, we found that all extant copies of said effort had been burned by incensed *TV Zone* readers, forcing us to start from scratch.

Ten years ago, we also noted that it was the job of the committed fan to rubbish any new *Doctor Who* before eventually accepting its merits in hindsight. However, this too has changed – thanks, we expect, to the series' sixteen-year absence from our screens and the fear that, if we fail to appreciate it enough, it might go away again. Now, you criticise a new episode at your peril, especially online. As you can imagine, this isn't much fun for us, so we've chosen to stick with the traditional approach. As a sequel, this book will of course be less funny than the original anyway – though we'd like to point out that, these days, it's far harder to raise a laugh simply by being unexpectedly rude or offensive. No – the spread of the Internet has allowed fans to be rude and offensive all the time, and quite taken the novelty value out of it. What's more, without Virgin's lawyers behind us, we're more worried than ever about accidentally committing a libel. That's why you won't see entries in this book for 'TOM'S PUTTING IT IN NOW', 'ANY OLD F**K WITH AN EQUITY CARD' or CHASBAPS. On the plus side, the net has spared us the chore of doing any actual research.

Our cover is, of course, the TARDIS; we thought it vital to maintain a consistency of design with our first volume. We couldn't use the brand new police box design, though, for obvious reasons, i.e., it was too fat. Our version hails from the Japanese translation of *Doctor Who in an Exciting Adventure with the Daleks*, which we're sure you remember well. On the subject of which: Once again, you'll notice we have made few allowances for people who are not already clued up to the eyeballs on *Doctor Who* minutiae. But don't worry, the less you understand the more you should congratulate yourself on not being a completely sad geek. Although, if you're reading this in the first place, perhaps you shouldn't be too smug.

Chris Howarth and Steve Lyons,
The Seventeenth Moon of Uranus, 2006

The Obligatory *Doctor Who* Episode Guide
Part B: TV Spin-Off Series
(Complete at Time of Writing)

K-9 AND COMPANY

1. A Girl's Best Friend

ABDUCTED BY THE DALEKS: Straight-to-DVD spin-off film, in which four women – Isabella, Sylvia, Anna and, in an obvious nod to the TV series, Barbara – are captured by Daleks, groped by their plungers and forced to engage in soft porn shenanigans for their entertainment. Admittedly, the ladies look great in the nak – but, oh, those Daleks in their shiny red and black liveries, now there's something to behold! Sadly, it seems the Terry Nation Estate were unhappy with this unauthorised use of their property, not to mention the complete lack of cash they were getting for it, and so had the film removed from sale. The producers sneakily tried to rebrand their pervy protagonists as Daloids, but no one was fooled. 'The reason the Daleks are still the most sinister thing in the universe,' said Tim Hancock of the Hancock agency, 'is because they do not make things like porn.' Well, apart from that time with Katy Manning, obviously. See also **BRAND OF THE DALEKS**.

ACORAH, DEREK: TV medium and 'Doomsday' guest star, whose on-screen possessions by the spirits of those who've passed on are surely conclusive proof that not only are ghosts* real, but that they all come from Liverpool.

ANT AND DEC'S SATURDAY NIGHT TAKEAWAY: Well... for a while there, it looked like ITV execs believed their own press, and thought they were filling their schedules with lightweight entertainment and

---

* Not Cybermen.

reality shows because they're popular, not because they're cheap. They seemed *that* confident in their diminutive Geordie stars to lure us away from a rare taste of proper imaginative drama on the other side. They were wrong, and their viewing figures were exterminated (copyright all newspapers). See also *CELEBRITY WRESTLING*. Not that anyone did. We may return to this subject from time to time. It makes us smile.

ANTI-AMERICANISM: Charge laid against the new series on the US Sci-Fi Channel's message boards – based, as far as we can tell, solely on the fact that, er, Henry Van Statten was American and he wasn't very nice. Yeah, and decades of British villains in Hollywood films count for nothing, we suppose. See also **BEANS ON TOAST**.

'ARE YOU MY MUMMY?': Possibly the scariest but certainly the most memorable line in the whole of the Christopher Eccleston Months. Perhaps next year, they could have a small child asking 'Are you my daddy?' as we imagine this would be equally terrifying but for very different reasons.

ARNOLD, DAVID: One of the UK's most accomplished composers. His scores have graced blockbuster movies from *Independence Day* to *Zoolander*, and his name is becoming synonymous with the James Bond franchise. He's also responsible for an array of TV themes, including the Tom Baker-starring *Little Britain* and the Tom Baker-starring remake of *Randall and Hopkirk (Deceased)*. So, why does his *Doctor Who* theme for Big Finish (not starring Tom Baker) sound like the tape got chewed in the recorder and half the tracks are playing at the wrong speed? Maybe he just popped it in the post without noticing, and the folks at BF were too polite to ask?

AS SEEN ON TV: Helpful blurb now often seen on the cover of *Doctor Who Magazine*. Well, you never know, some people might have failed to notice the press attention, the massive billboards on every street corner, the trailers before and after every BBC programme, the articles in every issue of *Radio Times*, etc, etc.

ASYLUM SEEKERS: We missed it the first time round – and no doubt writer Mark Gatiss did too – but apparently 'The Unquiet Dead' is a fascist diatribe against asylum seekers. We suppose if you scrutinise it closely, there is a sort of an analogy to be found: them bloody Gelth, comin' over 'ere, nicking our corpses...

AUTISM: Why all the fuss when Gary Gillatt suggested in *DWM* that some fans might have a touch of this condition? And for once, it wasn't the fans themselves who were moaning – because, let's face it, we were all too busy rearranging our shelves to keep our DVDs and books in chronological order.

No less a luminary than Colin Baker wrote to the mag to imply that none of the series' stars would have said such a thing, as Gary had claimed – briefly entertaining us with the notion of a companion-centred witch hunt to root out the offender. But the autism theory had been suggested before – two years earlier, in fact, when the Doctor was mentioned in Channel 4's poll of *The 100 Greatest TV Characters*. 'Everyone's slightly autistic in some way,' opined one of the talking heads on that show, 'that we all fix on something, a hobby – and if you're going to have a hobby, what a fantastic one to have, *Doctor Who*!' His name was Russell T Davies, and he was a writer. Wonder what happened to him?

AUTONS: C-List monsters, who, because their one party trick is smashing out of shop windows, can only be used every few decades otherwise it gets tiresome. They were considered big enough to open the revived series, though they didn't get a name check until the closing credits. They also featured in a trilogy of semi-pro videos, presumably because they were easier to build than B-Listers such as the Ice Warriors.

AUTOGRAPHS: A nonsensical idea if you think about it. Queuing for hours to get some celeb to scrawl his or her name across a piece of merchandise – we don't understand why anyone should do such a thing, and we've tried it hundreds of times in the hope of finding out. Could these be the same people who pack their Target books in plastic covers to stop them yellowing, and burst into tears when someone opens one and creases the spine? If so, what drives them to go handing a marker pen to anyone with the most tenuous connection to the story being novelised and uttering the words 'Write all over this, will ya?' All right, so asking Nicola Bryant to sign *that* page in the *Companions* book (not the JNT one) is good for a laugh (she won't), but...

Ultimately, these signatures are worthless too. A while back, forgery of signed comic books became so prevalent that dealers now only accept them if accompanied by certificates of authentication. All collections to date were thus invalidated – and as soon as someone realises the certificates are easier to copy than the autographs, it'll probably happen again. *Doctor Who* fans do have some breathing space, as there's no need for forgery to reach endemic proportions just yet. After all, unsigned copies of, say, Michael Sheard's many autobiographies are still far rarer than signed ones.

BAD WOLF: Instead of this cryptic message, wouldn't it have made more sense for Rose to have scattered the simple phrase 'Oi, go back and help the Doctor you stupid bint' subtly throughout her travels?

BADGERS, TALKING: Allegedly, their presence was Tom Baker's condition for appearing in a Big Finish audio. Athough if it were that easy, surely they'd have just given in? Tom also suggested a story in which the Fourth Doctor travelled the universe showing people his autograph book. Hmm, you can try a bit *too* hard to be eccentric, you know. It's probably a good thing anyway – not that we want Big Finish to, er, finish or anything; it'd just be nice if they slowed the releases down a bit and gave us a chance to catch up.

TEN Big Finish Series You May Be Tempted To Collect

1. *Dalek Empire*. Damn it, thought we could skip these, what with them having no one from the telly in them, at least not playing their TV characters. But then Nick Briggs landed the gig of voicing the Daleks in the Welsh series, and they went up a notch or

two in the authenticity stakes.

2. *Cybermen.* See above.

3. *The Sixth Doctor.* No, seriously, they're a massive improvement on the telly stories, helped by the fact that you don't have to look at that costume (barring the covers).

4. *Davros.* Give him credit, he's done well since embarking on a solo career, what with a sell-out stage performance and now a four-album deal. Soon he'll be able to afford all the rice pudding he could ever need.

5. *Gallifrey.* Well, if it's fanwank to allow Lalla Ward, Mary Tamm, Louise Jameson, John Leeson and Lynda Bellingham to reprise their *Doctor Who* characters at the same time, then bring it on.

6. *Sarah Jane Smith.* Between these and the *Gallifrey* discs, BF have really recaptured the spirit of the seventies despite a lack of Jon Pertwee and Tom Baker. But let's hope the eighties Doctors don't call it a day any time soon, else they might be tempted to produce *The Afterlife Adventures of Adric* or *The Perils of Peri.* Mind you, that last one could make a good DVD available from specialist shops – and we don't mean Forbidden Planet.

7. *Doctor Who Unbound.* See **UNBOUND**.

8. *Bernice Summerfield.* Someone once asked what the appeal of Benny was, and creator Paul Cornell replied: 'She's the humane one. She does domestic... she was the one who wasn't the player of games, but the seeker of scones... She's still generally placed against cosmic hugeness and villainous grandeur, and punctures those things by pointing out how divorced from reality they are.' Er, thanks Paul. We thought it was because BF kept pitting her against Daleks, Cybermen, Ice Warriors, Draconians, etc.

9. *Iris Wildthyme.* Eh-up, another spin-off of a spin-off. Anyone understand the appeal? Yes, in fact we do: it's Katy Manning doing t'reet funny accent, chuck.

10. *UNIT.* Nick Courtney's Brig and David Tennant, now that's a pairing we'd like to seen more of. Hint, hint.

BAFTAS: Never thought we'd see the day when a kids' show with farting aliens walked away with a BAFTA for Best Drama Series. But well done *Doctor Who*, it was well deserved and about time, even if Russell T and the BBC's Head of Drama Jane Tranter jointly denounced their failure to scoop more awards as 'snobbery' (sez the *Media Guardian*). As it is, the voting panel presumably overlooked the Bad Wolf arc. Another great achievement was Russell T's Dennis Potter Award for Outstanding Writing in Television. The voting panel presumably overlooked *Revelations*. Sorry, though, we can't believe it means all that much; not when the Doctor's crossover chums the *EastEnders* can walk away with Best Drama Serial. The voting panel presumably overlooked about a dozen other programmes.

BATTLES IN TIME: Partwork magazines are great, aren't they? Well, actually, let's rephrase that. Partwork first issues are great because they cost about 50p and come with fantastic supplemental free gifts; later issues cost about a tenner and come with nowt extra. And now *Doctor Who* has a partwork of its own, and frankly it's a disappointment. Instead of, for example, giving fans the opportunity to collect and build a full-size Dalek in only three thousand fortnightly instalments, publishers G E Fabbri have opted for yet another set of trading cards. They've at least tried to make them different, we suppose – #70 is a scratch 'n' sniff card featuring the fragrant aroma of a Slitheen bottom burp.

But, surprise, surprise, some cards are rarer than others and you're invited to buy extra packs to find the ones you don't get in the mag. Fabbri tested the sales potential of *Battles in Time* by giving it a trial run in the West Country (which was surely a risk; wouldn't it have been better to pick an area where more people can read?), which presented the rest of us with a horrible dilemma. What if the mag flopped and was never distributed more widely? Do we travel the length of the country and back every two weeks for the latest issues? Or pay outrageous prices on eBay? Although *BiT* is primarily about shifting trading cards, it's also got a *Doctor Who* comic strip (as if the world needed another), though at least this one has taken more trouble than most to tie in with the TV series. The first strips feature aliens from 'The End of The World' – have you heard the one about these tree fellas?

BBC THREE: Turns out it really was prophetic of 'The Daemons' to predict this digital channel decades before it appeared, even if what they envisaged was more like BBC Four. If only Letts and co. had foreseen a schedule stuffed with endless episodes of *Two Pints of Lager and a Packet of Crisps*, they'd have been spot on.

BEANS ON TOAST: Nutritious meal mentioned by the Northern Doctor. This exotic English dish has left American posters on the Sci-Fi Channel *Doctor Who* forum perplexed: 'What, beans? On toast!' So much so that Peter Kay could work a comedy routine around it (though we hope he doesn't). Cor, did we make this much fuss when they mentioned 'mac and cheese' in *Friends?* We did not.

BEASTLY BEHAVIOUR: If Rose had died in battle as the Beast suggested, he would have been responsible for one of the most diabolical acts in *Doctor Who* circles: giving away a right humdinger of a spoiler. The rotten bugger! Of course she didn't die in battle after all, so he was guilty of an equally heinous crime: reporting an unsubstantiated rumour posing as a spoiler.

BECKHAM, DAVID: English football royalty and future *Doctor Who* guest star, according to most tabloids at some point or other. Maybe one day it'll actually happen, just so they can stop printing it. Best rumour so far was that Becks and other showbiz luminaries would play plastic dummies of themselves in 'Rose' (two years ago, we'd have made a joke about Billie Piper being the only plastic celebrity the show needs but, fair dos, it turns out she can act). In the event, Becks's 'contribution' to that episode was limited to being dragged onto the competing *Ant and Dec's Saturday Night Takeaway* by a worried ITV. And we know how that turned out.

BESSIE: Congratulations are in order: Corgi Toys are celebrating their fiftieth anniversary in 2006. So what better time to say a big thank you to them for finally producing a little model of Bessie; of course it would have been more appropriate back in the seventies, but what the heck it's here now. You could even get one free with the special gift-set edition of 'The Three Doctors' DVD. What more could we ask?... Well, a little model of Jon Pertwee sitting in it would have been nice...

BIG BROTHER: Observant character in *Nineteen Eighty-Four*, George Orwell's vision of a dystopian future. Nice try, George, but you failed to predict anything as terrifying as the Sixth Doctor's costume, which appeared in the real 1984! Big Brother provided the inspiration for 'Inferno's' parallel Earth leader, whose photo adorned the walls there. The photo was actually of special effects designer Jack Kine, who had worked on the 1950s BBC TV adaptation of *Nineteen Eighty-Four* and was supposed to look suitably mean, though in fact he resembled the bloke in the Cadbury's Fruit & Nut adverts. Of course, *Big Brother* is also the Channel 4 programme that inspired Russell T to such an extent that he included a future version of it in 'Bad Wolf', using the actual diary room set and everything. We'd comment further on the Channel 4 freak show, but we've never seen it, honest. See also *ROOM 101*.

BIG FAT BOX SET: After the barebones, vanilla DVD releases, it was a fantastic idea to bring out the 2005 series in a box with loads of extras. Not such a good idea, though, to put five discs (a relatively small number) in a box the size of a small shed, stuck together with a glue stick that had had its top left off overnight. What's that you say, the Americans got theirs in a sensible box? No way! Still, it proves that series box sets are great, so how about one from the original series? In fact, Series Sixteen would be perfect what with the Key To Time arc running through all the stories. What's that you say, it's been out for ages but only in America? No way!

TEN Things That Could Have Been Included As Extras On The Series 1 Box Set

1. Those deleted scenes we kept being promised in the commentaries, carelessly misplaced before the discs were mastered – including the infamous burning sofa from 'Rose', excised under mysterious (and, we suspect, Health and Safety-related) circumstances.

2. *Wales Today*'s behind-the-scenes report, in which Christopher Eccleston was seen in 'costume' for the first time. Far more interesting in hindsight, because at the time nobody noticed. We all carried on speculating for days about how the Ninth Doctor might look, before the disappointing truth sank in.

3. *Doctor Who in an Exciting Adventure with Blue Peter*. See *BLUE PETER GARDEN*.

4. Any one of hundreds of BBC news reports about the return of the series, the casting of its lead actors, the departure of its lead actors, etc. Seems nowadays any excuse is good enough for the Beeb to plug its own shows under the guise of 'news'. Even their

News 24 channel carried a three-minute puff piece for 'Rose' on its day of transmission.

5. *Newsnight.* See what we mean? In the 9/3/05 edition of this hard-hitting news and current affairs show, the return of *Doctor Who* fitted neatly alongside items about Tony Blair's terror bill, the 'spread of democracy' in the Middle East and the methods of the Chinese police. Lovely, though, to see Jeremy Paxman dematerialising from the studio at the programme's end, in the time-honoured but still side-splittingly hilarious fashion.

6. There was even an extensive feature on BBC Two's *The Daily Politics*. *The Daily Politics*, for feck's sake!

7. Alternate soundtracks for 'Rose', including the Graham Norton one (see **NORTON, GRAHAM**), the one with the different music cues that was leaked onto the Internet and, for grown-ups, maybe one without the burp.

8. The episode of the UK TV Food Channel's *Great Food Live* on which Annette Badland dropped in to be a 'lunch guest' and discussed her *Who* work, but somehow resisted the urge to fart all the way through the meal.

9. Captain Jack's arse, we suppose, for those who like that sort of thing and so long as there are clear warnings on the menu screen. See **CAPTAIN JACK'S ARSE**.

10. An episode of *Celebrity Wrestling*. Just so we can relive the moment when we all changed channels.

BIG HAIR: The return of the 1992 *Doctor Who* pinball machine to a cinema near us prompts the observation that at first it appears the seven Doctors depicted are running away from Davros and the Daleks in a most cowardly manner. However, a closer inspection of their hippy-length locks makes it seem more likely they're just desperate to reach the barbers. The Fifth Doctor's golden mane, in particular, makes him look like a right girl. You know, at this juncture you feel it would be lovely if the volume you're holding was a lavish photo-packed coffee table book so we could back up the above with an illustration. But it isn't, so you'll just have to take our word for it.

BIKINI SHOT: Many moons ago, we interviewed Caroline John for *DWM* and were intrigued by her tale of how an atypical bikini-clad publicity shot landed her the role of Liz Shaw. She mentioned it again in the 'Inferno' DVD extras – but there was no accompanying still. If this photo is so hot that it got her a prime acting job without the need for an audition, we need to have a look for research purposes. So if it remains extant in any collection out there, please send us a copy care of the editorial address. Ta very much.

BILLIE: Conversations about *Doctor Who* can get quite confusing nowadays; sometimes it's only when someone mentions the length of Billie's skirt that you realise the topic is a Rose episode rather than a First Doctor one.

BIRDS OF PREY: Fans of 'The Invasion' might like to purchase this BBC thriller on DVD. Not only has it got Sally Faulkner in the cast, but some of the scenes were filmed on the steps outside St Paul's Cathedral. We didn't spot any Cybermen in it, but hey you can't have everything.

BLACK AND WHITE MINSTREL SHOW, THE: Hardly ever repeated for some reason – so no wonder few fans know about the episode in which the eponymous entertainers took a rocket ship to an alien world and met one of *Doctor Who*'s most popular monsters. Yup, it was a third TV outing for the great Alpha Centauri – and this time, we got to see him dance. A bit. Though, evidently, Alpha balked at wearing the customary black face paint. Now why hasn't *that* clip turned up on a DVD?

BLASPHEMY: The Daleks' opinion of the label 'half-human'. Coo, wonder if there's a real-life parallel going on there, then? For, truly, this has become the revelation of which fans dare not speak. Ten years, twenty-odd episodes, a hundred or so audios, a billion novels, short stories, comic strips and webcasts since the US telemovie, and so far not a mention. We've learned Vicki's and Ace's surnames (and arguably Polly's and Mel's, neither revealed on screen); we've learned who I M Foreman was (not that we cared); we've been treated to the returns of one-shot monsters including the Zarbi, the Mechonoids, the Zygons and the Nimon; we've seen a monster based on one line from 'The Brain of Morbius' (the Hoothi), and a character based on one line from 'City of Death' (Irving Braxiatel). The Doctor's past has been picked over in minute detail – and yet, of his alleged mixed ancestry... nothing. Not a sausage. C'mon, isn't it about time someone got to grips with this vexing issue? It only needs a line or two to clear up the whole thing, preferably on the telly. Our suggestions: 'I was half-human once, for a while. Don't know how that happened.' 'Phew, that was some post-regenerative trauma – didn't say anything daft, did I?' 'When I said "half-human", I meant in spirit.' 'What a lying git I was in my eighth incarnation.'

BLUE PETER GARDEN: Location of a titanic showdown between the Ninth Doctor and a Dalek disguised as a compost bin. Some fans may argue that this 2005 mini-episode isn't canonical – but Christopher Eccleston was in 'costume' and character throughout, and the Deus Ex Machina ending, in which he zaps his foe with a convenient *BP* badge, is perfectly in keeping with his other screen adventures. He could have been left the badge by Ace – and he could certainly have found his way to the *BP* garden, having visited it in the *DWM* comic strip 'TV Action'. In fact, all we need now is a story to explain how the garden came to be famously vandalised – probably by the Sontarans or Beep the Meep. Perhaps the First Doctor could place Steven Taylor undercover in the studio to get to the bottom of this, history's greatest unsolved mystery.

BRAND OF THE DALEKS: A fragile thing, it seems – hence the metal meanies' threatened no-show for the return of the programme that spawned them. 'We want to protect the integrity of the brand,' said agent Tim Hancock, who went on to accuse the BBC of trying to 'ruin the brand of the Daleks' – we can only assume by portraying them as evil killers again just as they were carving out a career in advertising (see **'PEACE AND LOVE'**). Anyway, the BBC put more money on the table, and those 'issues of editorial control' were ironed out, depriving us of the fond hope of a live-action outing for everyone's favourite Dalek replacements, *TV Comic*'s Trods. But see also **GAY DALEKS**.

BRITISH BOARD OF FILM CLASSIFICATION: Mary Whitehouse may be dead (hooray!), but her spirit lives on in the bureaucrats who banned kids from watching 'Dalek' on DVD. Its '12' certificate, they claimed, was justified by scenes in which the Doctor tortures his enemy. Except that, as DWAS representative David Bickerstaff pointed out on *GMTV*, he doesn't, he just tries to kill it. Which is obviously much better. 'We are concerned about role models for children using the sort of tactics that Doctor Who used against the Dalek,' said a BBFC spokeswoman. 'If that was transferred into the playground, it would be something we would want to tackle.' So, she's afraid that... what? Children up and down the country might electrocute their Dalek toys at school? Actually, that *would* be a tragedy. As for the Doctor, his 'violence and cruelty' are challenged in Rob Shearman's script ('You would make a good Dalek!') and shown not to be a solution – a point that appears to have been lost on the so-called experts.

BT TEXT: Service launched by British Telecom in early 2006, allowing text messages to be translated into spoken ones and delivered to land-lines. The *Doctor Who* connection here is that, for a limited period, said messages were read out by none other than Tom Baker. 'What appeals to me most,' said Tom, after spending eleven days recording every sound in the English language, 'is the thought that I will be bringing good news to people...' In practice, sadly, the service was generally used to make him repeat rude words or extracts from *Doctor Who* scripts to easily-amused fans. Still, shame on Big Finish for missing their best ever opportunity for a Fourth Doctor play. OK, so he may have sounded a bit monotonous – but, at least, in contrast to Jon Pertwee's *Zagreus* cameo, we'd have known what the hell he was saying.

BURJ AL ARAB HOTEL: A sail-shaped building in Dubai, it's almost identical to the hospital in New Earth and thus almost five billion years ahead of its time architecturally.

BURP: We're not sure why fans get so het up about this sound effect, dubbed onto a man-eating wheelie bin in 'Rose'. Can't they appreciate what was surely a tribute to the glory days of *Emu's Broadcasting Company?** And if that doesn't convince you, consider for a moment the sheer number of people through whose hands this scene must have passed and the enormous temptation with which each must have battled. Ultimately, a windless bin would have been like, ooh, an appearance of an outside loo that didn't have someone stumbling out of it, pants down, shaking his fist (observation copyright Rob Newman and David Baddiel, 1993).

BUSH BACKS DALEKS: 2004 headline in *The Sun* – referring, bizarrely, not to Mel (nor was it a description of those Katy Manning photos) but to President George W. The paper had got itself in a lather about the Daleks' absence from the new *Doctor Who*, and was claiming extremely high-level support for its campaign to 'save' them. Except that, er, Bush had said nothing of the sort; it was just an anonymous White House employer who'd muttered a useable quote when put on the spot. The *Sun's* campaign culminated in their wheeling a full-sized Dalek up Cardiff's St. Mary's Street during filming, only to be turned back before they could get near Billie. They still turned the event into a photo story, beginning with the caption 'Infiltrate! Infiltrate!' as their Dalek puts its

---

* Doctor Emu and the late lamented Rod Hull did indeed battle Deadly Dustbins back in 1977. And two years later, Doctor Eyes faced a bin in ITV's *End of Part One*, which was of course Geoffrey Sax's directorial try-out for the US telemovie. So, hardly an original menace.

not-so-cunning plan into action, then 'Remonstrate! Remonstrate!' as it's 'tin foiled' by a police officer, then 'Inebriate! Inebriate!' as it takes solace in the local pub, and finally, inevitably, 'Fornicate! Fornicate!' as it pulls a quartet of lap dancers.

CAMOUFLAGE: Not sure if those Torchwood troops were kitted out for action in the desert or the Arctic, but certainly not for fighting Daleks and Cybermen in a big warehouse full of flying saucers and stuff. Somebody should tell them before they end up getting killed.

CAPTAIN JACK'S ARSE: So, no alien worlds for the Ninth Doctor, but moons were OK. It took John Barrowman almost four episodes to become the first companion seen buck naked on screen – so imagine our non-surprise to learn that those *What Not to Wear* scenes were originally shot full-length from behind with Jack's weapons pouch (his gun butt?) in clear view. See also **GAY AGENDA**. Then the censors stepped in*, and demanded a re-shoot for the sake of the show's younger viewers. Then an attempt to air the original footage on *Doctor Who Confidential* resulted in a pixellated posterior. So, what did Russell T Davies do next? He announced that, instead of returning in Series Two as we'd expected, Captain Jack would get his own show, *Torchwood* – which would differ from *Doctor Who* in that it would be 'sexy' and 'for adult audiences'. Hmm, what could that possibly mean, then? At the time of writing, we haven't seen any *Torchwood* yet (because it hasn't been on, not because it clashed with something better or anything) – but we're putting our money on... ooh, let's say, thirty-two minutes in.

---

* We heard there was a crack edited out of 'The Empty Child' too, but it turned out to have been just a sound effect.

CARDBOARD CUT-OUT: Lovely Lis Sladen's opinion of Sarah Jane Smith in the original series. 'Each week,' Lis says, 'it used to be "Yes Doctor, no Doctor", and you had to flesh your character out in your mind – because if you didn't, no one else would.' Well, we can't argue with that, but is the new series really so much better? Perhaps Lis would prefer to be delivering lines such as Rose's vomit-inducing 'Can I just say how much I like travelling with you?'

CARDIFF: The new spiritual home for *Doctor Who* fans. And with the new series exhibition taking up temporary residence there, the city became something of a Mecca for said fans in 2006. Not only could they have a close look at the Space Pig and other props and costumes nearly as good, they could walk the streets and see the series' actual locations. They could carry their exhibition purchases down the same escalators as Jackie, take photos at the playground where young Mickey played (but hopefully making sure the kids have gone home first) – and apparently, they're queuing up to get married in St Paul's Church, seen in 'Father's Day'. Which is quite a surprise – how long have civil partnership ceremonies been allowed in church?

CARRY ON DOCTOR: Nice to see bubbly Barbara Windsor join Bernard Bresslaw, Peter Butterworth and Joan Sims on the all-too-small list of *Carry On* stars to have appeared in *Doctor Who*. Oh, and Jon Pertwee, we suppose. Shame it was such a brief (but brilliant) cameo for Babs in her role as *EastEnders* matriarch Peggy Mitchell. But, hang on, if *EastEnders* exists as a TV show in the Doctor's universe, it means 'Dimensions in Time' can't be real. Well, obviously we know it's not real, we int dat fick! What we mean is, thanks to 'Army of Ghosts', fifty per cent of original televised *Doctor Who* from the 1990s has been rendered uncanonical! Ooh yeah, so it has, cool. Pity there wasn't a scene in which Jackie sits down to watch the US telemovie.

CASSANDRA: Doom-prophesying computer from the fourth episode of *Red Dwarf VIII*, whom the cast of that series genuinely seemed to believe had been ripped off by *Doctor Who*. They even claimed, on a DVD commentary, that the Cassandra in 'The End of the World' looked like their version – a bit unflattering to actress Geraldine McEwan, who played the latter. In fact, the *Red Dwarf* Cassandra is far more clearly based on the doom-prophesying Trojan priestess of 'The Myth Makers'*, broadcast in 1965! The Dwarfers were also aggrieved about the similarities between their GELFs and *Doctor Who*'s Gelths. They may be completely different races with different origins, appearances and motiva-

---

* Oh, and of Greek myth.

tions, but, er, their names sound almost the same. Bet they're fuming even more, then, about those religious cat people!

CATS: When the Doctor claims not to be a cat person in 'Fear Her', it seems he's conveniently forgetting the selection of feline-themed badges that adorned his colourful apparel in his sixth incarnation. And who can blame him? On one of the myriad *Doctor Who* documentaries (we forget which) Russell T tried to justify the Sixth Doctor's outfit by suggesting it was indicative of over-the-top eighties style. Dunno where you used to hang out in the eighties, Russell, but even Leigh Bowery wouldn't have been seen dead in anything that outrageous.

CELEBRITY WRESTLING: Ooh, for a while it seemed ITV had brought out the big guns to challenge *Doctor Who* on a Saturday night. But it soon became evident that this programme was sadly lacking in the wrestling department and equally wanting where the celebrities were concerned. In fact the show was really *Gladiators* lite, but lacking the wit, sophistication, elegance and grace of its predecessor.

CHARACTER OPTIONS: What's going on here? Their action figures actually resemble the characters they're supposed to, and are the proper colours and everything*; likewise Product Enterprise's *Who* range is equally spot on. Doh! How can we be expected to make derogatory wisecracks about this stuff? More to the point, how can we resist buying it? It's so embarrassing, skulking around Argos waiting for their exclusive regeneration set to come back into stock – not to mention frustrating having to sift through hundreds of Doctor figures in Toys R Us trying to find a CyberController, particularly as some unscrupulous dealer has probably already been along, bought the lot and slapped an outrageous mark-up on the price. Come back Dapol, you're needed!

CHAVIC FIVE: Mentioned in 'The Long Game', and no doubt the planet of the Chavs.

CHICKEN BREAST ROMANA: You probably expect us to go on about the size of its portions. Well you couldn't be more wrong. In fact, we'd rather say nothing than stoop to such a juvenile level. Chicken Peri-Peri, on the other hand...

---

* Although, by the way, a Space Pig figure wouldn't go amiss. It could be used in conjunction with the *Pigs in Space* Swinetrek bridge set from *The Muppet Show* range, with our hero vying with Link Hogthrob for First Mate Piggy's affections.

CHICKEN, MR: An early inhabitant of 10 Downing Street, and a real historical person too. Now we don't mean to come over all educational or nuffink, but it's a mildly amusing name and we couldn't resist giving him a mention.

***CHILDREN IN NEED*:** What a pity Russell T chose to write a funny and touching scene to bridge the gap between the regeneration and 'The Christmas Invasion', thus passing up the opportunity to do 'Dimensions in Time' 2. Imagine it: the newly regenerated Doctor arrives in Albert Square* and is forced to confront evil local gangster and doting father Johnny Allen, who turns out to be the Master. Meanwhile, Pat Evans, Big Mo and Pauline unzip their massive body suits and are revealed as Slitheen. Rose, unsure about the new Doctor, feels so at home with the cockneys that she decides to remain in the Square, giving Kacey Ainsworth the chance to step in as new companion Little Mo, who, with the aid of her trusty sonic duster, will ensure the TARDIS is kept spotless at all times. Finally, for the dramatic drumbeat climax, Patrick and Dot admit to being Mickey's real parents.

CHIPS: Though reluctant to find fault with the episode that brought Lis Sladen back to us and had Giles from *Buffy* being really scary, there's one aspect of 'School Reunion' that just crashed through the boundaries of plausibility. There's no way that fat kid would have refused those chips just because he'd been told he wasn't allowed them – especially if they were free. They'd have had to chain the porker down!

CLASS 4G: *DWM*'s focus group of ten and eleven year-olds from South London's Ibstock Place School, upon whom they conducted cruel experiments involving enforced viewing of 'Terror of the Zygons' and 'The US Telemovie with the Pertwee Logo' (the latter before its UK broadcast). Why they didn't show them serial 4G, 'Pyramids of Mars', is beyond us – perhaps they were worried about setting a precedent and having to subject the poor kids to 'The Creature from the Pit'** the following year. The young audience concluded after 'Zygons' that the odd Skarasen is forgivable if the script's strong enough, and their verdict on the telemovie was that the odd plot hole can be overlooked if the effects are good. So, basically, they'll just watch what they're given. They hated that kiss, though.

---

* *EastEnders* cast correct at time of broadcast but, as ever, subject to change. See DEAN, LETITIA.

** Did you see that issue of *DWM* where Jonny Morris showed the infamous Erato-fellatio scene to John Beyer, Mary Whitehouse's replacement as head of Media Watch UK? He missed the point entirely, opining that it was too violent. This is why we should never, ever listen to a word these people say.

Alarmingly, *DWM* editor Gary Gillatt confessed that both stories were shown unedited, even though both were cut for their home video releases and the telemovie still got a 12 certificate. Ten years on, six former 4Gers are in prison for firing guns at telephone boxes, while the other four killed each other with pitchforks. Actually, that was a lie – and until it happens, we'll trust the judgement of Gary and Class 4G's teacher over that of the BBFC (see **BRITISH BOARD OF FILM CLASSIFICATION**).

'CLAWS OF AXOS, THE': The only, repeat, only episodes of old *Doctor Who* released on DVD during transmission of the first series of new *Doctor Who*. And yeah, yeah, we know the Restoration Team did something clever to the picture, and the BBC wanted to keep the new and old brands separate, but still – with all those new viewers potentially interested in exploring the show's rich past, was it really necessary to tell them to sod off quite so emphatically?

CLIFF: If you thought Captain Jack was the first companion designed for the gay demographic, you'd be wrong. Before becoming Ian, the original male companion was to have been called Cliff (after Cliff Richard who, for the benefit of our American readership, was the king of Rock 'n' Roll). In the original documentation, Cliff was described as 'physically perfect... a gorgeous dish'. And this was written by a man called Bunny!

CLOCKWORK ROBOTS: Clockwork in the 51st century? That kind of thing really winds us up!

CLOM: Another planet with a north.

COLOUR*: Exciting feature promised on the DVD release of 'Spearhead from Space' – though, apart from a few splashes of beige, it's difficult to spot any. Indeed, the Third Doctor himself is presented entirely in monochrome. This is because most viewers in Britain (i.e., everyone apart from the Queen and a few rich bastards) were still using black and white sets in 1970 and wouldn't have noticed the difference anyway. That said, as Third Doctor DVD releases go, 'Spearhead' was a first-rate choice (and not just because it's only a four-parter, though that's certainly a bonus) – but black-and-white-averse viewers looking for a titanic clash between Jon Pertwee and those unnamed monsters from 'Rose' should probably wait for 'Terror of the Autons', by which time other hues had been subtly integrated into the programme.

---

* For the benefit of American readers, this unfamiliar word means 'color'.

COMPANION ACADEMY: *Totally Doctor Who*'s theatre of child cruelty. Cadets were totally forced to face their greatest fears (which, in most cases, seemed to be vegetables on plates), read out some long words and walk totally barefoot across a load of mouse traps, or so they were totally led to believe. It was all a swizz anyway, as winner Louise never got to replace Rose as totally promised. And we aren't convinced that answering questions on *Doctor Who* episodes is totally the best way to pick the perfect sidekick, anyway.

TEN More Appropriate Tests For Next Year's *Companion Academy*

1. In the first episode, each cadet should demonstrate one skill that makes them different from the others, e.g., they're a computer programmer, they studied botany, they got the bronze. They must then never, ever, mention this skill again, on pain of expulsion.

2. The mouse trap test suggested that companions should follow orders. We beg to differ. The cadets should be left in a studio and told to stay put. The last one to wander off would be the loser. Or they could go to a museum, like Van Statten's, where only those thick enough to touch the exhibits would survive into the next round.

3. All cadets should be tested on their aptitude with a mobile phone. The quicker you can text your friends, the quicker you can save the world.

4. Emotions are important to the new-look companion – so just as, in the old days, the cadets might have been asked to scream, now they should be required to blub convincingly.

5. In Russell T's *Doctor Who*, more than any other, the companion has to cope with sudden, indiscriminate death. Therefore, the judges should study the cadets' reactions when somebody is brutally slain in front of them. We nominate Barney.

6. David Tennant should come into the studio, and – rather like John Barrowman working his way through the pack of ladies in *How Do You Solve a Problem Like Maria?* – be snogged by each cadet in turn, both girls and boys. Only those with a real spark would stay in the game, though tongues would be optional.

7. The male cadets should take off their shirts, so the judges can rate their chests. Those who show other bits as well get bonus points. However, there's unlikely be an equivalent test for female cadets.

8. The all-important 'reaction to the deadly killing machine' test. Do you (a) run up a few steps and then stop to hurl pithy insults at your pursuer, apparently oblivious to the fact that, even if you're correct in your unfounded assumption that it can't fly, it can certainly *shoot upwards*; or (b) run like hell?

9. As it's important to keep the series grounded, the cadets should bring their families and friends into the studio to be judged on whether they're interesting or not.

10. The cadets should line up while the judges decide which of them best resembles the illegitimate daughter of Paul Cornell. We're not sure what this would prove, but that Chrissie from the first series would have walked it.

CONNOLLY, EDDIE: 'Pardon me, officer, but the mother-in-law's had her face sucked off by the telly and now she's stomping about upstairs like a mindless zombie. Can you help?' We're guessing at the actual words Eddie used to 'grass up' Granny, of course, but that must have been the gist of it. So: an evil fascist, or just a concerned son-in-law?

CROWBAR: Useful implement for levering mentions of Torchwood into every Series Two script. See also **SHOEHORN**.

'CURSE OF FENRIC, THE': THE SPECIAL EDITION: We might have been more convinced by this 'movie version' if they'd put together a new, more appropriately Hammer-esque title sequence for it, rather than sticking with the usual stupid silver-faced, winking McCoy one.

CYBERMAN SHOP DISPLAY: Produced to promote the release of the Series 2, Volume 3 DVDs – and, unlike the extras-free discs themselves, this fantastic life-size, 2-D Cyberman – fashioned from genuine cardboard – would make a splendid addition to any fan's collection. Indeed, we'd have asked our local W H Smiths for theirs when they'd done with it, if only someone hadn't knocked its head off. It was probably a Dalek what done it, though we can't say for sure as we weren't there at the time.

CYBERMAN VOICE CHANGER MASK: Seems a waste of perfectly good electronics to us, as surely any normal mask would suffice to make the wearer's voice appropriately indistinct, bordering on inaudible. They look pretty good, though – and the added bonus of this toy is that, once the kids are bored with pretending to be Cybermen, the handles can be sawn off, it can be painted red and gold, and they can play at being Iron Man instead.*

CYBERPORN: So far, this commonplace term can't be applied to any spin-off films in which a bevy of nubile, nude nymphets discover how formidable the Cybermen's iron wills are before indulging in a spot of 'mat-munching. It's very disappointing.

---

* We were all set to compile a list of things the clunky new Cybermen reminded us of: the face and chest unit are reminiscent of various Iron Man designs, of course, while the bottom half has a resemblance to the Maria robot from *Metropolis*. There was also a Japanese character someone pointed out to us, but we've forgotten its name so it doesn't count. But that was about all really, so a more original design than we first thought. Well done!

DAEMOS RISING: A late entry into the pantheon of unofficial film spin-offs. Almost uniquely, this one features no stars of television's *Doctor Who*, not even Sophie Aldred! We might have let them off for that if the Daemon had looked a bit like the one the Third Doctor and Jo saw off, but it didn't.

DALEK ART EXHIBITION: Imagine our disappointment when, upon entering a gallery expecting to view paintings of space battles between Daleks and Mechonoids, all we found were pictures of green cartoon monkeys. They're the work of artist James Marshall, who's supposed to be quite famous – but if that's the case why does he need to call himself 'Dalek' and lure in unsuspecting, gullible *Doctor Who* fans? Hancock's ought to have a word. See also **WALLINGER, MARK**.

DALEK CAKE: As concocted by dear old Valerie Singleton on *Blue Peter* four decades ago. The item resurfaced on the DVD of 'The Dalek Invasion of Earth', but the vital Dalek taste test was excised on the orders of – you guessed it – the Hancock agency. What we *should* have seen was the metal meanies lamenting Val's 'insult to the Daleks', expressing their worry that 'All the Earth children will laugh at the Dalek master race' and consequently exterminating the offending repast. But, oh no, that would have meant presenting the Daleks in a comedic context and we all know this must never, ever happen. Or, given one Dalek's opinion that the cake contained 'too much chocolate', perhaps someone was just afraid for their KitKat revenue. Personally, we believe Hancock has a point: the Dalek brand has now been ruined by the suggestion that anyone can get away with baking an insulting cake in their image. Just look at *Totally Doctor Who*, where viewers are totally always sending in their own efforts without fear of reprisal. You can even buy one in the shops, with a voice chip buried in it. Though come to think of it, this could be part of a Dalek revenge plan, in which the laughing Earth children all choke to death.

DALEK MASK: Available to cut out of *Doctor Who Adventures #7* – and bloomin' convincing it is too, oh yes.

DALEK PLEASURE PROBE: It had to happen. For over forty years now, we've known that it just... had to happen. And it has. 'The Dalek pleasure probe,' says the Fantasy Supplies website, 'is 14" long, incorporates a handle for ease of use and the unique design provides extra G spot stimulation.' It's also 'flexible & waterproof'. And it looks a bit like a Dalek eyestalk. We don't even want to think about it.

DALEK STAMP: The metal meanies from Skaro were awarded the ultimate accolade when one was chosen to appear on a Royal Mail stamp. You could even get a postcard of it so you could stick it on and send it to yourself (and the stamp image was turned into a coaster for cups, though we're not sure of the post-related significance there). The advantage of collecting Dalek stamps is that they're smaller and easier to store than, say, a radio controlled Dalek, especially as there's only one so far. In fact we'd be quite tempted to collect all the stamps based on British television shows if only they hadn't elected to go with *Emmerdale* rather than *Coronation Street* to represent soaps in the ITV 50th Anniversary set, which was just plain wrong.

DALEKS VS. CYBERMEN: Oh, please! Come on guys, that's just so flipping obvious. It's like the zenith of fanwankery, it's... fantastic. Do it again! Do it again!

DAMAGED GOODS: When the writer of this 1996 New Adventure was announced as the guiding light behind the revived *Doctor Who*, there were those who feared the entire series would be set on a council estate and the scripts riddled with references to homosexuality. But as it turned out, less than half the series was set on a council estate and the gay references were few and far between – though the Doctor quoting from *The Lion King* was a bit too overt for our liking. See also **GAY AGENDA**.

DANCING ON ICE: Having suffered a knockout with *Celebrity Wrestling*, ITV might have been expected to submit, but instead decided to play it cool. Not only did they keep their next Saturday evening extravaganza well away from *Doctor Who*, they bunged in a couple of *Who* celebs for good measure. It was an ice try from John Barrowman, but he under-achieved really and probably deserves a demotion from Captain. Bonnie Langford, on the other hand, proved that she really is the most talented woman in show business – but although she melted the judges' hearts, she was frozen out by cold, unfeeling public voters.* We thaw it coming, but did she really deserve such a frosty reception? Come on folks, time to forgive and forget, surely. Admittedly, Mel was a misjudged career aberration, but Violet Elizabeth – that was just good acting.

TEN Other Shows That Have Featured *Doctor Who* Actors In Memorable Roles

1. *Marple* (or should that be *Tommy and Tuppence?*). Bonnie again, here cast as the mother of a precocious, annoying child actress. Hmm, do you think they were trying for irony there?

2. *Sea of Souls.* Glasgow is visited by ghosts, demons and other supernatural beings on a weekly basis, yet the parapsychology team maintain a Dana Scully-like scepticism throughout. It's like *Scooby-Doo* in reverse. Then Paul McGann turns up as an immortal wizard-type character and suddenly they're all believers in magic. What a convincing actor he is!

3. *To Serve Them All My Days.* Matthew Waterhouse's other acting job.

4. *Survivors.* Patrick Troughton guest-starred in an episode of Series Two, the one where it became quite like *The Good Life* only without the benefit of the jokes or Felicity Kendall's bottom.

---

* Some people claimed she had an unfair advantage as she was a professional dancer. Plus, there was all that time she spent living on Iceworld.

5. *Tenko.* Louise Jameson was especially memorable in this. For her fine performance, of course – why else do you think we mean?

6. *The Tomorrow People.* OK, so maybe we do usually like topless appearances from *Doctor Who* regulars, but not Peter Davison!

7. *Blake's 7.* Features what is undoubtedly Colin Baker's finest hour (well, fifty minutes really) in a BBC TV science-fiction show.

8. *Strange.* Ian Richardson apart, this was a perfect example of how not to make a Saturday evening telefantasy show. Though in its favour, Tom Baker did appear in one episode.

9. *Mayo.* The eccentric Sylvester McCoy should have felt right at home in this bonkers BBC detective series. He played the Reverend Beaver, and the other characters thought it was funny because the Reverend looked a bit like a beaver (the make-up was rubbish). We on the other hand think the word 'beaver' is amusing for other reasons.

10. *Second Coming.* We haven't seen it as apparently there are mentions of Manchester City. However, all you need to know is that Russell T Davies writes and Christopher Eccleston stars; now there's a pairing that's been known to divide opinion.

DASILVA, HOWARD: Some American bloke whose allegedly amusing voiceovers were added to Tom Baker episodes in the US to recap the story for viewers with short memories. You could have seen them on the DVDs, but it seems the Restoration Team involved with the releases turned them down on the grounds that they aren't in fact amusing at all, preferring instead to commission the likes of *Eye on… Blatchford.* What's that you say, they're on the Region 1 discs? No way! To be fair, the DaSilva stuff *is* brain-meltingly awful. But that's not the point. We *want* to see awful material from the archives, because we enjoy laughing at it. Why else do you think we bought 'The Web Planet'?

DAVIDSON, PETER: A surprise return for the misspelt Fifth Doctor, on *Totally Doctor Who* of all programmes. We almost missed it, still reeling in shock as we were from 'John Pertwee'. Totally wrong, totally unacceptable. See also **'SOME OF THE BEST DOCTOR WHOS'.**

DAVIES EX MACHINA: Mischievous phrase made up by us, in the hope of having it adopted by the fan community. It means... oh, you know what it means. But for the sake of balance, see the following list.

TEN   Pre-Russell T Deus Ex Machinas

1. The First Doctor's ring, as good as anti-plastic any day – though it's ninety-eight episodes before we learn of its 'certain properties', and after it's fixed the TARDIS lock on Tigus they aren't mentioned again. 'Yes,' says Steven, 'but what properties has it?' 'Now, I don't want to discuss this any more,' explains the Doctor.

2. So, you've defeated the Doctor, you've got Earth where you want it – what next? Well, if you're Azal of the Daemons, you might want to kill yourself because some daft bint says something you don't understand. Better, surely, to have killed the daft bint.

3. The Hostile Action Displacement System. Phew, what luck that, the one time the Doctor remembered to set this device, the Krotons attacked his TARDIS with a big gun. Though if only he'd remembered that it's indestructible anyway, he could have saved himself the fuss.

4. We covered hexachromite gas in Volume 1 – except to say that at least its presence was established before it was used. Unlike the convenient big 'story off' button that somehow managed to pitch the Sycorax leader off his ship in 'The Christmas Invasion'.

5. And what was that handy Gods of Ragnarok-destroying amulet doing lying around on Segonax anyway? Almost as silly as leaving the firing controls for the UK's arsenal of deadly missiles lying around on the Internet.

6. Even five Doctors couldn't keep Borusa from his prize of immortality – and, as the whole thing was a trap anyway, they may as well not have tried. Can't help thinking, though, that

had the mad Time Lord played the Game of Rassilon by the rules, he'd have reason to feel aggrieved at its outcome. It's the Bad Wolf scenario again... What on earth was wrong with a simple, unambiguous instruction like 'Don't stick your finger in my ring'?

7. All that fuss trying to keep the Hand of Omega/ Nemesis Statue from the Daleks/Cybermen, and it turns out the Doctor had pre-programmed it to backfire on them all along. So, why didn't he just step back and let it happen?

8. 'An Aquafein!' cries the First Doctor. 'Use your ray pistol!' And Ian does just that, saving the day with a weapon he happened to have about his person. What a copout! And quite frankly, the rest of the stories on those Give-a-Show projector slides are little better.

9. The Rani's meant to be super-intelligent, right? So, why would she make such a boneheaded mistake as to put a second time brain in her computer, when anyone with a basic grounding in science knows that'll make it explode? And once again, multiple Doctors don't have to do a thing, just watch.

10. And finally, we're trying to lay off the telemovie this time round, we really are – but it does have the biggest, most appalling Deus Ex Machina in the history of, well, fiction. The TARDIS – the *TARDIS*, of all things, the show's biggest constant – turns out to have the power to reverse any defeat the Doctor could possibly suffer and resurrect dead companions to boot. No point worrying about those cliffhangers in future, then! At least we can be sure the new series would never do anything as daft as... oh.

DEAN, LETITIA: Blimey, we're forced to eat our words of ten years ago, because she's returned to *EastEnders* – and left and returned and left and returned, etc. – making it seem that the soap's producers are hell-bent on fitting 'Dimensions in Time' into continuity when 2013 comes around. All right, so they killed off Kathy – but that hasn't stopped them in the past.

DEAN, LETITIA [addendum]: Bugger it, now they've gone and let Wendy Richard leave too. That's about it, then, for 'Dimensions in

Time's' credibility. But isn't that always the problem when the creators of speculative fiction attempt to predict the near future? They invariably get it wrong, and people notice! Hence the moon still being in its orbit and why, even in 2006, we're still using cars and buses instead of zipping around the solar system in sleek spaceships to the accompaniment of classical music. Russell T's probably got the right idea, actually, going for such ridiculously futuristic settings that no one's going to contradict him for a very, very long time. Nevertheless, we sincerely hope that, five hundred thousand years from now, someone will update this book if only to point out that *Big Brother* is no longer being broadcast.

DEATH COMES TO TIME: Webcast adventure, which, despite starring Sylvester McCoy and therefore – even at the time – being set before the events of hundreds of books, comic strips and audios, not to mention a certain telemovie, took the small liberty of killing off the Doctor.

'DELETE': Lacklustre attempt to give the Cybermen a catchphrase to replace 'Excellent!' and compare with the Daleks' frankly incomparable 'Exterminate!' With homeless people providing the raw material for the first of the new Cyber-breed, perhaps 'Can you spare some change?' might have been another, more terrifying possibility?

DENT, ARTHUR: The Tenth Doctor seems to know this other dressing gown-clad space traveller. In which case, if they both inhabit the same universe, why hasn't Earth been blown up by the Vogon constructor fleet and why isn't everything funny? Unless, of course, the Doctor is familar with the film version of Arthur, which would explain everything.

DICKENS, CHARLES: The *Observer* took issue with the Northern Doctor calling him 'Chazza', asking why the Time Lord had to act 'like a spoilt Salford brat in need of a slap to put a stop to his cheeky chappie wisecracking and irksome insolence?' We were more bothered about the fact that Chazza was left to save the Earth from the Gelth while the Doctor hid cowering in a darkened room.

DILDO, THE PLANET: Still makes us laugh. See also ORGI.

DISCLAIMERS: Mealy-mouthed lawyers' statements that spoil the illusion of BBCi's spoof *Doctor Who* websites. 'We apologise for any inconvenience caused,' says one such, on the UNIT site, 'if you thought this was a real website dedicated to fighting off alien invasions.' See also WHOISDOCTORWHO.CO.UK.

DIVERGENCE UNIVERSE, THE: Big Finish-created realm where there was no concept of time. At least, that was the idea. In practice, it just seemed nobody had bothered to invent the clock. Ironically, for anyone attempting to listen to the Eighth Doctor audios set here, it seemed that time did actually stand still.

DOCTOR AAAWOOO!: Not one of their best, but this was *The Sun's* headline when they revealed the Doctor was to encounter a werewolf in 'Tooth and Claw'. Since *The Sun* does seem to be the most reliable source for exclusive *Doctor Who* news of late (no, really*) we'll let it go this once.

DOCTOR OOOOOO!: The *News of the World's* nickname for the Doctor when they printed pictures of the 'time bawd' kissing Rose – with tongues too, apparently. Conveniently, they forgot that Rose was possessed by Cassandra at the time, as that would have been far less salacious. Not to be outdone, *The Sun* suggested that 'Flash Doc's a Time Lewd', who wanted 'to show new assistant Freema Agyeman his... Tardis (sic).' Why? Because they'd snapped a photo of him from behind with his coat billowing open a bit. Journos really love this kind of stuff, don't they? Obviously not getting any at home.

DOCTOR SCREW: 2006 series from the UK Adult Channel, with a trademark-flaunting taxicab logo and the strap line 'Shagging His Way Through Time'. Doctor Screw comes to Earth in pursuit of his nemesis the Mistress, and takes over the body of rock star B Nasty as 'his true alien form would be far too minging to get any real action'. Together with sexy young reporter Holly, he travels in his portaloo-shaped time machine, the TURDIS (what else?). The Doctor's 'cheeky catchphrase' is 'Cunnilinguist!' and he has a knack of escaping the Mistress's traps – 'often by f**king his way out!' We only have proper terrestrial channels ourselves, so we can't add much more. However, the show's website promises episodes in which the Doctor 'blags and shags his way across medieval England, occupied France, the stone age, a massage parlour in outer space and even a f**k fest in a black hole'. No alien planets, then? And yes, for all you shippers out there (see **SHIPPERS**), Holly *does* end up 'dropping her knickers' for him.

DOCTOR WHO ANNUAL 2006, THE: Almost a return to the good old days, with its nostalgic mixture of original prose adventures, features and a comic strip. Though sadly, Panini didn't quite pull it off; their mistake was including some half-decent stories, forcing the BBC to step in...

---

* And no sooner do we write these words, than they have to go and spoil it. Zoe Lucker as the Rani, indeed!

DOCTOR WHO CONFIDENTIAL: BBC Three behind-the-scenes documentary series in which Russell T Davies tells us how lovely everything is, writer/Big Finish guest star Andrew Collins reveals his extensive knowledge on all things *Doctor Who* (especially quarries) and some bald man keeps turning up for no adequately explained reason. And that's about it really, week after bloody week.

DOCTOR WHO DUVET COVER AND MATCHING PILLOW CASE: Finally, more than twenty years after the Peter Davison wallpaper came out, the *Doctor Who* fan's room-cum-shrine can be complete* and the dedicated geek can sleep soundly wrapped in Daleks. It should go without saying, though, that these are made for single beds only.

DOCTOR WHO – THE LEGEND: Large coffee table book – in fact stick some legs on it and it could *be* a coffee table. It is quite possibly a well-written and informative tome, but we may never know, because the layout is so vile it makes it impossible to read.

DOCTOR WHO WATCH: Not only a regular *Radio Times* feature shamelessly plugging the new series, but also a timepiece available from all reputable dealers in *Doctor Who* merchandise – and no doubt the other sort too, mentioning no names. So there you have it, two entries for the price of one.

DOCTOR'S AFFECT, THE: Not by any means the most amusing mistake in a *Doctor Who* book – but it takes a special kind of publisher to get one right up there in the title. But hold on, according to our dictionaries, 'affect' *can* be a noun. It can mean a 'feeling, emotion, desire, esp. as leading to action'. Do you think that might be what they were getting at after all? No, we don't either.

DOGS: Another word that didn't exist ten years ago. Well, obviously it did, but it didn't stand for Digital Onscreen Graphics. Now, DOGs are all over digital TV channels on the grounds that viewers might be too stupid to remember what they're watching without a prompt. We say 'all over', but of course we only mean over the programmes – they disappear for adverts, cos they're far more important.

And there is one other surprising exception. When BBC Three repeat *Doctor Who* these days, it's without an intrusive reminder of the channel's name in the top left corner. Which is interesting,... Though quite honestly, we're not sure what to make of this one. Do we laud a sensible

---

* There are of course *Doctor Who* curtains available too, not to mention those Dalek and Cybermen light shades that came out a while back.

result of the application of fan power? Or despair at the sad gits who have nowt better to do than complain about a logo obscuring a tiny part of the episodes they've no doubt already recorded off BBC One and bought on DVD? Hmm, wonder what we have to do to make the DOGs take a walk for *Confidential* too...?

DR LOO AND THE FILTHY F**KING PHALEKS: What, more porn already? This one is from Doll Theatre, whose other tie-ins to popular BBC TV shows include *Snatch of the Day*, *Only Fools and Arses* and *Horny City Hospital*. Manchester-born Alicia Rhodes plays Dr Louise Flangebatter, McKenzie Lee her companion Quimberly Dickmore and Karla Romano their 'shagbot' Kay 9 (though Doll Theatre's website misspells her surname 'Romana' – intentionally, we'd like to believe). Their time-travelling toilet, the TURDIS (hang on, this sounds familiar) takes them to Skrotum 4, where the Lady Sodomi has created an army of evil sex machines. The Phaleks, complete with 'E-jac-ulate!' catchphrase, are realised as wobbly pink Alpha Centauri-shaped creatures with all the usual attachments plus one. There's even a bit of a *Flash Gordon* crossover in the persona of Sodomi's husband, Emperor Minge the Merciless, who plots to turn Earth sex mad with a sex ray.

Ultimately, this female Doctor eschews a violent solution in favour of a peace deal, with the Phaleks staying on as their former enemy's playthings. And, happily, a thrilling cliffhanger promises a sequel outing against the Cidermen. *Dr Loo and the Filthy F**king Phaleks* is an R18 film, but a cut-down 18 version is available for the sensitive. It's called simply *Dr Loo and the Filthy Phaleks* – so clearly far more wholesome.

DR WHO STARS' STALKER TERROR: *Daily Star* headline in April 2006, after BBC Wales Online encouraged fans to show up during filming, track down the series' stars and post sightings and photos. And hilarity ensued.

DRAMA QUEEN: See **BAFTAS**.

DWARFS: Oh, honestly! One offhand quip in Russell T's Production Notes for *DWM*, and you get the *Mirror* proclaiming what they tactlessly called a dwarf 'shortage' caused by the simultaneous filming of *Doctor Who*, *Harry Potter* and *Charlie and the Chocolate Factory*. Though maybe there was something in it after all – those Oompa-Loompas all looked suspiciously similar. Suspiciously like 'The Talons of Weng-Chiang's' own Mr Sin, in fact.

EARS: What Chris Eccleston himself says he brought to the role of Doctor Who – which is nice, as it saves us being insulting. What a pity then that more wasn't done with them. Instead of relying on the sonic screwdriver all the time, perhaps the Doctor could have had super hearing like the Bionic Woman or something.

EASTER EGGS*: Marks and Spencer's released a couple of these in 2006. The Dalek one was very nice, but the TARDIS egg looked too much like the Series One DVD box set packaging, and thus provoked feelings of anger and resentment. But at least it contained chocolate instead of Eccleston episodes – which was arguably a plus, depending on your point of view – and as such any plans to keep it unopened, uneaten and in pristine mint condition were doomed to failure.

EBAY (RANT #1): A great place to find those elusive pieces of merchandise, but not necessarily to snap them up at bargain prices. The Internet has opened up a whole new world of shopping for those geeks who wouldn't normally venture out from the safety of their bedrooms in their parents' houses, never mind go to a comic mart or a convention dealers' room. Consequently, competition is fierce. For example there was the story of the Pertwee Annual that made the local papers because

---

* There's also another kind of Easter egg on the *Doctor Who* DVDs – though, on the whole, they're pretty dispensable and barely worth the few seconds of your life it will take to press left on the remote in order to find them.

it sold for three figures, and astonishingly it wasn't even the rare pink one!

Then there was the American who put his favourite issue of *Marvel Premiere* (#60 featuring 'City of the Damn... erm, Cursed') up for auction with a minimum bid of $1,000. This easily amused guy was patently having a laugh, but that didn't prevent irate fans from e-mailing him to tell him the true value of the comic. To which he replied: 'You Brits are a fun bunch of gentlemen. I have enjoyed the repeated condescending e-mails I have gotten... You [Brits] have spent more time on this ad than I did... You have way too much time on your hands and need to find a hobby or make some friends to fill that gap in your social life that leaves you so so bitter.' Not all the mails he received were along the same lines, though. For example: 'I might consider bidding on this item if the shipping cost wasn't so high.' Now, that's comedy!

Less funny were the unscrupulous people who thought it OK to buy up all the Dalek Battle Packs they could find prior to Christmas 2005 and flog them on eBay for inflated prices – it was like the Furbies all over again! And how is it that, with the plethora of *Doctor Who* goods available for auction, that final 'Masterplan Q' Nestlés wrapper is still so flipping hard to track down?!

EBAY (RANT #2): Ebay is also, of course, our biggest and best source of missing episode lies, beating out that loon who used to offer 'The Evil of the Daleks' and suchlike in the classified ads of various newspapers. Best eBay scare so far was when film cans of 'Mission to the Unknown' and 'The Roof of the World' turned up for sale from an evidently reputable dealer. How excited we all were – until we noticed that the reels (chucked out in the seventies) were labelled with bits cut out of the *Doctor Who Programme Guide* (1981). Apparently, they'd been mocked up by a fan to see what they might look like, and sold on without his knowledge by a relative. Don't you hate it when that happens!

ECCLESTONE, CHRISTOPHER: Commonly believed to be the first incumbent of the big fat TARDIS, most shockingly by Billie Piper in her autobiography. Could be worse, though. When the *Daily Mail* announced Chris's casting, they misspelled his name 'Bill Nighy'. Later editions of the paper corrected the cock-up – though they left in the one about Alfred Molina guest-starring in an episode about Joan of Arc.

EDIBLE BALL BEARINGS: For a time, it seemed the Doctor admired humanity for its indomitable pioneering spirit, its courage and determination and other such laudable bollocks. Turns out he's very, very easily pleased.

E-JAC-U-LATE: If the Dalek in 'Dalek' downloaded the entire Internet, there must have been a lot of hardcore porn floating around its synapses. No wonder its balls fell off! See also **DR LOO AND THE FILTHY F**KING PHALEKS.**

ELLISON, HARLAN: Talented, multi-award-winning SF writer and self-professed *Doctor Who* fan. He certainly knows what he's talking about, so when he delivered his verdict on the new series, we thought we'd better listen. And these were his words of wisdom: 'Why in the world WOULDN'T you call it "Season 27" when it's the twenty-seventh season of DOCTOR WHO?' Ummm... OK, a well-reasoned argument, Mr Ellison. But surely you meant to say 'Series 27'? It is a British programme, don't you know.

EMERGENCY TEMPORAL SHIFT: Since the cool Black Dalek obviously survived 'Doomsday', wouldn't it be a good idea to say balls to *Torchwood* and give Sec or whatever he's called his own spin-off series? In fact if Tracy-Ann Cyberman survived too, they could team up and go on the run from Torchwood and UNIT – it could be a bit like *Max and Paddy's Road to Nowhere*, only funnier.

EUROVISION SONG CONTEST 2006: Shows just how huge *Doctor Who* has become these days, when even Eurovision can be won by a group of big Finnish monsters. Um... worked better out loud, that one.

EVANS, CHRIS: See BECKHAM, DAVID, although obviously the difference in this case is that they'd have to step over our dead bodies chained to the doors of the new Cardiff studios to get this ginger git in front of the *Doctor Who* cameras. Hopefully it was just the presence of Evans' ex-wife in the show (Billie, if you didn't know) that started off this particular flight of fantasy – for surely he couldn't *really* have been considered for the role of the Devil in 'The Satan Pit'? Even the tabloids could only swallow that one by imagining the titular Pit as a nightclub with Evans the chirpy host in a devil suit. Though who knows – maybe, at the time, that seemed a more likely scenario than an actual visit to another world...?

EXPLODING KNOCKERS: Proving that being a scientist isn't always a boring job, top tit experts have discovered that breast implants explode in outer space. While their research has no obvious ramifications for *Doctor Who*, if it precludes Jordan ever being cast in the companion role, it will have been worth it.

EXTERMINATION EFFECT: It's not that we don't appreciate the painstaking efforts taken to source the very best quality pictures for the DVDs – but you'd hope the people doing the sourcing would notice when those pictures *aren't the right ones*! Particularly when they're missing what was, in 1988, just about the most lauded special effect ever seen in the programme. What's that, you say, the scene is intact on the Region 1 release? No way! How about at least squeezing a clip into one of those interminable making-of things on a future Dalek-related DVD? Sheesh, between this and the whole fiasco over Beatles rights, it looks like we're never gonna get shot of those rusty old Dalek video tins!

FACE OF BOE: Some find him enigmatic; personally we think he's a bit big-headed.

TEN Stunning Revelations The Face of Boe Might Make To The Doctor If He Can Ever Be Bothered

1. 'I'm your father.'

2. 'You're my father.'

3. 'Martha is really Arthur.'

4. 'I'm also a bit dubious about Captain Jack.'

5. 'I love blinkin', I do.'

6. 'The butler did it.'

7. 'Remember that bird Rose? I've 'ad 'er...'

8. '...and your little dog too.'

9. 'Your logo is crap.'

10. 'I love you.'

TEN

And While We're At It, Here's Ten More (Starting With a Popular One With Fans)

1. 'The Time Lords aren't all dead after all. Some of them, including the Master, escaped into the Void. In fact I wouldn't be surprised if they hadn't shifted their entire planet (formerly known as Gallifrey) over with them.'

2. 'Elvis, on the other hand, *is* dead.'

3. 'I prefer to watch *Star Trek*.'

4. 'Here's the secret recipe for Vimto. Use it wisely.'

5. 'I killed Kennedy.'

6. 'When I say "Boe", you say "selecta".'

7. 'You think the face is big, you should have seen the size of my...'

8. 'I think I've finally worked out what Bad Wolf means.'

9. 'I've still got all me own teeth you know, young man.'

10. 'Knock, knock...'

FAMILY AUDIENCE: How lovely to see this term once more associated with *Doctor Who* – and indeed, Russell T has pulled out all the stops to give the revived show universal appearance. There are Daleks and zombie grannies for the kids, soapy council flat scenes for the mums, Billie and fart jokes for the dads, Dr Sato for the teenage nerds, Adam and Captain Jack for everyone else. Just a shame the BBC publicity people couldn't have been more helpful; seems they couldn't make up their minds from one minute to the next whether the show was suitable for under-eights or not. Shadow Education Secretary Tim Collins leapt into the debate, arguing that the programme was 'perfectly appropriate for six year-olds.' He was presumably referring to the complexity of some of the plots.

FANS, WHIRLING: Let's be fair, it takes a lot of guts to repeat a science-fiction cliché after it's been so famously parodied. Post-*Galaxy Quest*, it's impossible not to ask *why* that reset switch was on the other side of the spinning death devices in 'The End of the World'. Did this significant flaw not show up when Platform One was designed? What about the poor technician who booted up the computer to start with? And yet, surely Russell T can't have meant for us to watch the end of 'The End of the World' without hearing Sigourney Weaver shrieking: 'This was a badly written episode!'...could he?

FANWANK: No, nothing to do with Billie at all, or even Captain Yates. Only online *Doctor Who* fandom could invent a derogatory word for tie-in fiction that's, er, aimed at its target audience. The argument goes that excessive references to the Doctor's past put off new viewers in the eighties, so any references to the show's rich history are now taboo and Gary Russell's knackers should be hung from the nearest lamppost for *Divided Loyalties*. It would have been awful, after all, if the legions of non-fans who were surely reading the EDAs and PDAs had been confused and put off them – you know, like they were by mentions of the Time Lords, K9, Eternals, the Nestene Consciousness, Cybermen, Daleks, two hearts, regeneration, mummies, Draconia, Daemos, UNIT[*], Sarah Jane, International Electromatics, polycarbide, the Isop Galaxy, anti-matter monsters, Zeus Plugs, Jamie, etc., etc. in the new TV series. See also **'IT'S NOT BEING MADE FOR US'**.

---

[*] To be fair, some fans did complain about UNIT's resurgence in 'Aliens of London' – but why, for Tom's sake? They're a significant part of the programme's history; to write them out in favour of a new outfit that do essentially the same thing would be ridiculous, wouldn't it?

FATHER CHRISTMAS: So, now the Doctor claims to have been this mythical figure, too. We just don't see how he could have pulled it off, even back when he was a fat bloke in a colourful costume. Though at a pinch, maybe he just filled in one year for his old *TV Comic* chum? Even so – waiting till the dead of night to sneak into the home of the twelve year-old girl he intends to make his companion and leave her gifts... that's called grooming, mate!

'FATHER'S DAY': Right audience, listen up. This is deeply moving stuff, OK? You will be sad; you will go on an emotional rollercoaster ride; you will cry real tears at the poignant ending – and that's an order! Alternatively, those viewers less inclined to be manipulated by a kid's drama show might just think, 'Come on Pete, jump under the bloody car already, we all know you're going to!'

Ultimately it's all rendered much less sad anyway by Pete's return, albeit as a parallel universe version. As a dad himself, not to mention a seasoned traveller across dimensions, you'd think the Doctor would be more clued up on what constitutes fatherhood – despite the Doc's claims, other-Pete was in no way, shape or form Rose's dad, being, as he was, in another universe at the time of conception. Not even the CSA would have grounds to counter that argument.

'FEAR HER': Or *Paperhouse*, as the film version was known – written by Matthew Jacobs of telemovie fame, but don't let that put you off. If you'd rather read the story in book form, seek out *Marianne Dreams* by Catherine Storr. While we're on the subject, fans of 'The Girl in the Fireplace' might enjoy *The Time Traveller's Wife* by Audrey Niffenegger.

FHM: Billie Piper is the eleventh sexiest woman in the world according to this popular lads' mag. This may not quite be the accolade it seems however; certainly the majority of the opposition seem to be women for whom multi-tasking is the ability to pout and wear a bikini at the same time. Though judging by the photos, some of them weren't quite able to manage both.

'FICTIONAL ALIEN': Wikipedia's description of Beep the Meep, the second greatest character in *Doctor Who* comic history after the Dalek Emperor from *TV21*. Worryingly, the website sheds no light on who the real aliens might be and where they could be hiding.

FIFTH DIMENSION: The existence of this 'mischievous dimensional force' in a filing cabinet at *Doctor Who Weekly* was their excuse for cocking up a succession of photo files on the stars of the series they were supposed to be covering in depth. Sundry misprints aside, they confused Debbie Watling with her character and introduced her to fandom as Deborah Waterfield. But she got off lightly compared to Jackie Lane, who gained an entire new life. Apparently, Jackie was born in New York, the daughter of an immigrant Russian family, and worked there post-*Who* as Jocelyn Lane. She also gained an impressive list of false film credits. But, hold on, what's this? The whole story appeared again in Gary Downie's *Doctor Who Cookbook*. Surely that couldn't have happened were it not the absolute truth? Confused, we naturally turned to the ultimate *Companions* book for clarification. Doubtless, John Nathan-Turner would have much to say on the subject of the most important companion of all: the one who solved those niggling problems of viewer identification and set a precedent for young, contemporary female assistants in the TARDIS. And, after hours of poring over Dodo's entry in the volume, we can state with confidence that, er, Jackie Lane played her. We'll take a wild guess, then, that the later write-up in *DWW*'s *Gallifrey Guardian* – which accompanied the fifth dimension 'joke' – is accurate. Even if they spelt her name 'Jacki' throughout. And said she was hired by producer 'John Wild'.

TEN More Vaguely Interesting Things We Found While Flicking Through Old *Gallifrey Guardians* In Search Of Inspiration

1. Seems there was a bit of a fuss, back in the day, about the cover to Target's novelisation of 'The Keys of Marinus'. The BBC had no colour photos from the story, and their black and white ones weren't detailed enough to provide proper reference. Fortunately, a solution was at hand. 'With the help of some off-monitor photographs from the original BBC episodes,' revealed the *Guardian*, 'Target are able to produce a cover for "The Keys of Marinus" faithful to the 1964 serial.' And with thirty years' hindsight, we can see what that cover depicted: The TARDIS. In space.

2. After his exploits in 'The Star Beast', Beep the Meep was sentenced to three thousand years' imprisonment by Judge 'Stickler' Scraggs. Though, according to 'Star Beast II', he was out on parole after fifteen. Typical!

3. Sorry, did we say ten? We meant two. Got bored after that.

'FIVE DOCTORS, THE' – THE SPECIAL EDITION: Not the most auspicious start to the DVDs. The actual broadcast version of the story would have been nice, as would some extras. But never mind that – the thing really playing on the mind of the typical collector is the fact that the sleeve design is unique, and not at all uniform with the releases that followed. Fortunately, there was an opportunity to download a standardised cover, not available in the shops, from the BBC website – presumably to dissuade irate fans from burning down BBC Worldwide for another day. See also **SPINAL CRAP**.

TEN Things That Could Go On A Decent Re-Release Of 'The Five Doctors'

1. The actual broadcast version of 'The Five Doctors'. Along with a new commentary.

2. The Region 1-only commentary for the 'Special Edition', in which Terrance Dicks explains why the actual broadcast version of 'The Five Doctors' would have been better. (What's that, you say, the spine was uniform with the other R1 releases, too? No way!)

3. Peter Davison and Richard Hurndall in costume on *Blue Peter* with that *Doctor Who* minibus thing.

4. Intros and cliffhangers from the four-episode version of the story, as actually broadcast.

5. Some footage of the Longleat twentieth anniversary event.

6. Outtakes, such as the one where the Dalek gets lost and the one where Bessie stalls and Jon Pertwee swears.

7. Peter Davison and Richard Hurndall meeting Wogan on *Children in Need*. They didn't half get around in that *Doctor Who* van!

8. Patrick Troughton's rare TV interviews to promote the actual broadcast version of 'The Five Doctors', on shows like *Nationwide* and *Breakfast Time*.

9. Ohh, loads of other twentieth anniversary stuff from *Saturday Superstore*, *Pebble Mill*, etc.; really, there's no shortage.

10. And, whether we want one or not, a newly-made talking heads making-of documentary featuring everyone who was involved in the actual broadcast version of 'The Five Doctors' and has so far managed to stay alive.

FOOTBALL: The Northern Doctor can receive this in the TARDIS (notice he didn't call it soccer?). Some fans have suggested that since he has a Mancunian accent he must be a Manchester City fan, which is balls on so many levels. Not least because he actually has a Salford accent, so is likely to be a United supporter if anything.

In real life, Christopher Eccleston does indeed support Manchester United. His character in *Cracker* did likewise – but in *Hillsborough* he played a Liverpool fan, and in *Second Coming* Manchester City was the club of choice. Well, God Junior *would* side with the helpless and downtrodden... Wisely to avoid alienating sections of the audience, the Ninth Doctor's preferences were left unspecified. We don't know which football team he supports either.

FORD, ANNA: TV newscaster who, according to OnDigital's listings magazine for November 1999, played the Doctor's very first travelling companion.

FORRESTER, ROSLYN SARAH: A companion created for the New Adventures. No surprise, then, that she carried a gun and hopped into bed at the drop of a zip. Roz was fated to leave the NAs in Ben Aaronovitch's *So Vile a Sin* – but that book was delayed, leaving us to find out the news when the series' next instalment opened with her funeral. And people complain about spoilers for the new series! Fans of uniform book spines were also incandescent when *So Vile...*, now completed by Kate Orman, finally turned up with the anachronistic new cover format; the one on which the words *Doctor Who* weren't mentioned at all. As an exercise in easing readers into the new, Doctor-less, Benny-led books, this was... No, it was a bloody daft idea.

FORTY-FIVE SECONDS: Strange how one vaguely anti-Iraq War line in 'The Christmas Invasion' – you know, the one about not letting the US president take the UK to war – got so much press attention, while this far less subtle jibe from 'World War Three' seemed to slip by unnoticed. Strange, too, to hear the punch line delivered by a nineteen year-old chav who, lest we forget, couldn't name the Prime Minister in the preceding episode. Strangest of all, though, was the idea that the United Nations would sanction use of weapons based on nothing more than proof of an alien threat to the world. Twelve years of meetings and a stiff letter to the invaders – followed by a slightly less stiff letter – would be more their style. See **UNIT**.

FREEMAN, RICHARD: Britain's leading cryptozoologist and author of the book *Dragons: More than a Myth*. He is critical of boffins, in particular Richard (Mr Lalla Ward) Dawkins, who dismiss the possibility of undiscovered creatures without leaving their 'ivory towers' to look for them. Mr Freeman makes a compelling argument for the existence of strange animals, but what originally drew him to this fascinating subject? '*Doctor Who* when Jon Pertwee was in the role.' Oh. OK, Richard. Erm, see ya.

FREEVIEW: Supposedly fully functional Digital TV platform on which, nevertheless, the words 'Press the red button now to hear a commentary' rarely apply to frustrated *Doctor Who* viewers. Events that have bumped the show off the interactive channels include Wimbledon, World Cup Football, a Red Hot Chilli Peppers concert and the Chelsea Flower Show. So it's comforting to know that, as popular as the series has become, in some quarters the old pecking order remains.

FRIDAY NIGHT PROJECT, THE: Channel 4 show that's only of interest because Billie Piper once appeared on it; she played Rose in a spectacularly unfunny *Doctor Who on Ice* sketch. Co-host Justin Lee Collins was the bescarved Doctor – though with Collins, it's not so much 'who' as why. Why is this annoying man on television?

FROST, MURIEL: Possibly the first non-TV *Doctor Who* character to make it into the actual series – that is, if the soldier with the name tag

'Frost' seen in 'Aliens of London' was indeed the Captain Muriel Frost of *DWM* comic strip fame. Supporting evidence comes from *Doctor Who Classified! A Confidential 3-D Dossier*, which discusses the events of the 2005 series from the point of view of a General Muriel Frost. The only problem being that half the *Dossier*'s events occurred after the TV character's death.

FRY, STEPHEN: Once-mooted TV series writer and past webcast guest star. According to MPs, he's also the actor they most wanted to become the Ninth Doctor. How do we know this? Because BBC Worldwide polled our elected representatives to celebrate the show's fortieth birthday, and 130 of them had nothing better to do than respond. Close runners-up were Alan Rickman, Bill Nighy, David Jason (?) and, er, Tom Baker – though with a total of seventy-eight names put forward, there couldn't have been that much between the lot of them. Some MPs tried to be funny, but failed, nominating Jeremy Paxman, William Hague and Iain Duncan-Smith. Zoe Wanamaker and Joanna Lumley were the most popular female nominees – presumably among members who'd never seen the series, else they'd have known the Doctor is a man. It was even suggested that Kate O'Mara, having played both villain and companion, could complete the Hat Trick. 95% of MPs had heard of the Daleks (so, who the hell elected the remaining pig-ignorant 5%?), but only 45% of the Sea Devils and 33% of the giant maggots. 28% claimed to have hidden behind the sofa when the show was on – and now we trust them with our nation's defence – while Tom Baker was the runaway winner of the favourite Doctor category. 5% found the series 'addictive, compulsive or unmissable'; in other words, they were Scarf-Wearing, Fanatical Whovian Bastards. So, some valuable market research there. Not that the BBC were actually making *Doctor Who* or anything at the time...

THE COMPLETELY UNOFFICIAL
ENCYLOPEDIA

GALLIFREY: To lose it once to a great Time War, in the books, could be considered bad luck. To lose it twice...

GARLICS: Clove-headed metal meanies who did battle with the Chuckle Brothers* in their hilariously-titled stage show *Doctor What and the Return of the Garlics*. In the interests of research, we did consider going to see this production, but then we thought balls to that, it'll be rubbish, probably only marginally better than *The Ultimate Adventure*.

The thin brother (whichever he is) played the Doctor in a Tom Baker scarf (still, surprisingly, a ubiquitous symbol of the TV programme) and, in another frankly pathetic copyright-dodging attempt, travelled in a red telephone box. Although in fairness, the boys did have the good taste to use a variation of the Pertwee logo on their posters, rather than that new thing.

---

* Russell T Davies used to write for Barry and Paul years ago. Which possibly explains a few things.

TEN

Proper *Doctor Who* Stage Plays With Licences and Everything, and Their Respective Claims to Canonicity

1. *The Curse of the Daleks* (1965). Some people crash land on Skaro, and one of them wakes the Daleks in the hope they'll make him King of the Universe. With hilarious consequences. Hmm, well, it features the Thals, and refers to Unispace agents and compressed water – both from the spin-off universe of the sixties Dalek annuals and comic strips, and we certainly want to believe *they're* canonical. So... **Canonicity Rating: 8**

2. *Doctor Who and the Seven Keys to Doomsday* (1974). Typical fare from Terrance Dicks, set on the planet Karn – but not 'The Brain of Morbius' one, so points off for that. And it starts with the Third Doctor regenerating into Trevor Martin, so it sort of contradicts the rest of the Tom Baker era too. **Canonicity Rating: 4**

3. *Recall UNIT, or The Great T-Bag Mystery* (1984). We still don't know what the hell this was about, even though one of us sat through it. But it featured a race of Dalek mutants called Dragoids, who disguised themselves as, er, men in drag. And Richard Franklin and John Levene played both themselves and their characters. In skirts. **Canonicity Rating: 2**

4. *Hot Ice '86* (1992*). The Sixth Doctor and Peri finally made it to Blackpool for an eight-minute-long rink-based adventure with the Daleks, the Cybernoids (whatever they might be) and best of all, an ice-skating dinosaur. Points off for recasting the leads, though presumably two less, er, front-loaded actors were required. **Canonicity Rating: 7**

5. *The Ultimate Adventure* (1988). The actual first meeting of Daleks and Cybermen, the difficulties of which we covered in the previous volume. **Canonicity Rating: 5**

---

* Naw, only joshing. It was 1986.

6. *The Trial of Davros* (1993). Put on by the Hyde Fundraisers several times, with two different Davroses albeit both off the telly. So, it's the 'Ultimate Adventure' problem all over again. No reason to believe, though, that the most recent version – staged in a proper theatre and everything – couldn't have happened. **Canonicity Rating: 9**

7. *The Empress of Othernow* (1994). Staged by Huntington Drama Club and attempting, like other spin-offs before it, to atone for a shameful omission from the TV stories by featuring an Earth on which the Roman Empire never fell. This particular paradox was caused by Cybermen arsing about in the time stream. Featured a new companion called Gwen. **Canonicity Rating: 7**

8. *The Tomb of the Cybermen* (1998). Hmm. Hard to fit this production, put on by students at Oxford Brookes University, into television continuity, as surely the Fourth Doctor – played by Richard Laming and accompanied by, er, Ben and Victoria – would have remembered having this adventure before. **Canonicity Rating: 3**

9. Pat Troughton claimed he didn't like 'shouting in the evening', and apparently he wasn't keen on stage acting either. So, even if he was around today, he most likely wouldn't have played the Second Doctor in the Portsmouth-staged remakes of *The Web of Fear* (2000), *Fury from the Deep* (2002) and *The Evil of the Daleks* (2006), produced by various theatre companies but all featuring Nick Scovell as a bearded Doctor. But at least the companions in all three were Jamie and Victoria. **Canonicity Rating: 6**

10. And if you thought it was cheating, including three plays in one entry – well, we're counting *Hellblossom*, *Vox Dei* and *Warsmith* (2000-2002) as a trilogy too, so there! Portsmouth is obviously the place to be for theatre-loving fans; apart from the adaptations above, it was the only place to see the Ninth, Tenth and Eleventh Doctors in action with their companions: Sha'atara, a Valkyrie from New Asgard; Prince Karnak of the Jocastan Imperium; and Penny11, a robot from HappyWorld. Mark Wright, David Huntingdon and Mike O'Doherty played the Doctors – so it's probably a good job they stopped before they ran out of incarnations. Plenty of continuity references, though, to such stories as 'The Seeds of Death', 'Genesis of the Daleks', 'An Unearthly Child'... but hang on, what's this? A

mention of the Doctor's wife in the first script? Aaaargh! Fanboy anathema! **Canonicity Rating: 0**

GATISS, MARK: We must have missed this piece of legislation, but it seems a law was passed forbidding any British cult/telefantasy programme to be made without a contribution from Mark.

GAY AGENDA: What gay agenda?

GAY DALEKS: They cruised the universe in their TURDIS long before either Dr Loo or Doctor Screw thought of it. They had a robot dog called KY before Lily Savage used the same joke. And their battle cry, of course, was 'Ex-sperminate!'. But their proposed animated series for BBC Three fell foul of Dalek agent Tim Hancock – who even cited it as proof of the BBC's brand-ruining master plan (see **BRAND OF THE DALEKS**). Funny, that, as the original Gay Daleks sketches, for *Victor Lewis-Smith's TV Offal* (a Channel 4 show) were seemingly approved by his agency. A disappointed Lewis-Smith went on record with the suspicion that 'what really irritates them [Hancock's] is the depiction of a Dalek as a friend of Dorothy.' Quite right too – as it was firmly established in 'Remembrance of the Daleks' that the Daleks and Dorothy don't get on at all well. The writer got his own back by later claiming, in an *Evening Standard* review of 'Dalek', that he'd been reminded of his own creations when 'a butch, burnished gold Dalek, all chained up in what looked like an SM bondage dungeon [was] enthusiastically tortured by a man in a rubber suit.' Perhaps that's what the *Sun* meant when they revealed the new blinged-up metal meanie to the world with the headline 'Puff Dalek'.

GEEK: Apparently, in between TV adventures, Mickey spent all his time at his computer, updating Clive's website (see **WHOISDOCTOR-WHO.CO.UK**) and sending other Internet users hacking into computer systems to thwart alien schemes. And here we all thought he was a cool guy!

TEN Famous Mickeys

1. Mickey Mouse. Very funny, but no Donald Duck.

2. Mickey the Monkey. British comic character whose amusing simian antics couldn't prevent the cancellation of *Topper*.

3. Mickey Dolenz. Drummer with the Monkees, who later went into TV production and was responsible for...

4. Metal Mickey. A robot but also a complete twat. Makes you appreciate K9 all the more.

5. Mickey Rourke. Suppose he can be quite cool.

6. Mickey the idiot from *The League of Gentlemen*. Played by *Who* writer Mark Gatiss, obviously a man of many talents. Well, two at least.

7. Mickey from the song by Toni Basil, as featured incessantly in *Doctor Who* documentaries of late.

8. Mickey Spillane. The late, great creator of Mike (not Mickey) Hammer.

9. Mickey Rooney. Diminutive Hollywood actor.

10. Erm, how about Mikey the taciturn scouser from *Big Brother*, close enough?

GENESIS ARK: Crikey, no wonder the Time Lords got wiped out if they wasted valuable fighting time cramming millions of POWs into a prison ship and then let the Daleks go and nick it, the pesky blighters. As for their security arrangements... so, *any* time traveller could open the Ark just by touching it? Even though the Daleks can, er, time travel? And claiming they can't touch is no good, is it? Not when we all saw that Dalek in 'Dalek' exposing itself to the world. Clearly, all a Black Dalek had to do was sucker a single minion out of its casing, clamp its writhing body against the Ark, and it would have been Open Sesame.

GOLDEN AGE: The result, in the UK, of Harriet Jones's three terms as Prime Minister. Until the Doctor stuck his beak in and changed history, ending her premiership months after it began in a fit of pique.

GOOD AND EVIL: Twin concepts (or maybe it's just the words) that Russell T is reluctant to use in Welsh *Doctor Who*. This is lovely, because it means we don't have to feel guilty about rooting for the bad guys when the Doctor and Rose are being particularly irksome... C'mon you The Beast!

GOODING JR., CUBA: Academy Award-winning actor who, in the parallel universe of 'Rise of the Cybermen', shared Jackie Tyler's birthday, 1st February. Yet, in the real world, Cuba was born on 2nd January 1968. This must have been a clever attempt to suggest subtle differences between the two dimensions – as surely someone couldn't have just looked up Cuba's bio on the net, seen his date of birth cited as 1-2-68 and forgotten that the Americans write their dates the other way round to us...?

GRADE, MICHAEL: Former BBC One Controller, who cancelled *Doctor Who* in 1989 and has professed his hatred for it on a regular basis since. Grade sent shockwaves through fandom by being appointed BBC Chairman just after the return of the show was announced. He never really had the power to axe it, this time – but that didn't stop five desperate publicity-seekers – er, we mean Members of Parliament – from writing to him to demand he keep his hands off.

Ultimately, though, this is a story of redemption – for, despite having vowed not to watch the new-look series, Grade later confessed to having been won over by it. Or maybe he's just hoping we'll all leave him alone now. Fat chance of that. See also **LISTED PROGRAMMES** and *ROOM 101*. Oh, and did you know that, during his time at London Weekend Television, Michael Grade also cancelled *The Goodies*? The twat!

GRASKE: Considering the interactive digital adventure 'Attack of the Graske' featured possibly the most PC family in the history of television, it's unfortunate that the evil Graske was portrayed as an alien of restricted growth. By constantly including evil characters such as dwarves and leprechauns, films and TV are simply reinforcing stereotypes that are probably not even true. This is most unfair to short-arse actors.

GROUND ZERO: Comic strip in which *DWM* 'delinked' – to use a made-up word much bandied about at the time – their continuity with that of the New Adventures, by killing off Ace where Virgin insisted she'd grown up into a space bitch called Dorothée Sorina-McShane. To confuse things further, BBC Books reckoned she was always called Dorothy Gale anyway. Or was that Dorothy Gale McShane? We're not sure. Though we can certainly dismiss the idea that she took over from the dead Time Lords (see *DEATH COMES TO TIME*). Perhaps she just grew older gracefully, called herself McShane for a while, and became a mentor figure to Hex. We have similar problems with Peri, as neither Marvel nor Virgin chose to respect Philip Martin's wish (in the *Mindwarp* novelisation) that she return to Earth and become a wrestling agent for Yrcanos. And let's not even mention the alternative timelines of the Eighth Doctor (oops, too late – see **McGANNISTS**)!

For a time there, between TV series, it seemed the various spin-offs were slugging it out to become the One True Continuity. Which wouldn't have been so bad if they hadn't constantly referenced each other, e.g., Bernice in BF audios, Evelyn having conflicting leaving scenes in an audio and a PDA, Muriel Frost in everything. BBC author Lawrence Miles even attempted to lock the New Adventures away in a 'bottle universe', but had to suggest that some of them had, er, leaked out a bit. And ultimately, what was it all for – as the Welsh series has urinated over the lot of 'em anyway? How many 'return of Sarah Jane' stories was that we heard disappearing into the void of non-canonicity after 'School Reunion'?

GUINNESS (BOOK OF) WORLD RECORDS: So, now they're listing *Stargate SG-1* as 'Longest-Running Sci-Fi TV Show (Consecutive)'? Really? Their pathetic excuse is that *Doctor Who*'s multiple suspensions and cancellations bars it from this category *even though* its initial uninterrupted run from 1963 to 1985 still knocks spots off *Stargate*'s puny efforts. So, if *Stargate* were ever to be resurrected as a TV movie, it would presumably be disqualified too, and have to pass its crown on to *Star Maidens* or something.

Hmmm... 'Dear Mr Guinness, I note that a Mr Daniel Baraniuk holds the world record for sitting on top of a pole for 196 days. However, I believe he sat on other poles prior to this, and so cannot be described as a "consecutive" pole-sitter. I would therefore like to claim this record for myself, having tried it this morning and managed two seconds before I fell on my arse.'

Ah, well, maybe we shouldn't grumble. After all, in 2001, Guinness credited *Doctor Who* as the world's biggest book series 'based around a single principal character'. But even if they'd done a recount this year and remembered to include the New and Missing Adventures this time, that would make around four hundred titles – compared to over three thousand starring Germany's SF hero, Perry Rhodan. Justin Richards will have to start writing a lot faster if he wants to catch up with that.

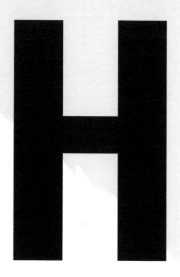

'HAD A DRINK. HAD ANOTHER DRINK. LET THAT GINGER MAN OFF *THE BIG BREAKFAST* GET ON TOP OF ME. DID *DR WHO*': The likely text of Billie Piper's much publicised autobiography, according to speculation in the *Metro* newspaper. Not only is this disrespectful, it's inaccurate. They missed out an entire chapter: 'Made some pop records.'

HAINING, PETER: We haven't heard much from him lately – wonder if he's still the world's leading authority on *Doctor Who?*

HAM ACTOR: An uncredited Jimmy Vee played the Space Pig. No disrespect meant mate, it's a kind of pun.

HAND OF SUTEKH, THE: Oh, well done, *DWM* readers! Give you a chance to vote for the next DVD release, and what do you pick? 'The Trial of a Time Lord' (cos it would have forced 'em to release a series box set, no other reason)? The actual broadcast version of 'The Five Doctors'? Any Graham Williams episodes? Nope. 'Pyramids of Mars' it is – perhaps the one story that, given its ever-present popularity and the predilections of the Restoration Team, was guaranteed an early showing anyway. Though at least it ended that tiresome debate on whether Sutekh's bottom-fondling moment should be left intact or pointlessly butchered.

Anyway, why do some fans imagine that the airbrushing of an extraneous hand might elevate a story to *Star Wars*-like levels of gloss and sophistication? Look, we don't mind the odd CGI spaceship so long as we can still watch the original hubcaps – but how do you explain a Bottom-Groping Version and a Non-Bottom-Groping Version of an episode on the menu options?

HEADMASTER: Ho ho, yes, Anthony Head as 'the Headmaster'. Must be the Master then, yes? Well... no. Which is what happens when fans get too used to keeping an eye out for cunning anagrams like Torchwood, James Stoker, Mr Seta, Queen Angvia of the House of Silcitor, etc., in *Doctor Who*. Though Headmaster = Head, Master... That wouldn't have been the most cunning one ever, would it? And we're not sure there's ever been a major casting decision based on a simple word play before. This is why Big Finish have never asked footballer Gary Neville to play Dalek creator Yarvelling in an audio. Or actor John Axon to portray, er, an Axon.

'HE'S YOUR BOYFRIEND': Trouble is, thanks to Eccleston's ambiguous delivery, we'll never know if this was true or not. It's possible that, after Adam Mitchell fainted, the Doctor was just saying 'He's your boyfriend so it's up to you to look after him.' But it sounds more like he's doing a sarcastic Newman and Baddiel-style riff, i.e., 'You see that Adam? That's your boyfriend, that is.' On the subject of that faint, Adam – who had previously spent time examining alien artefacts, encountered a deadly Dalek and been for a spin in a space-and-time-travelling ship that's bigger on the inside – falls over melodramatically because he's in a not-very-futuristic space station. Surely the only shocking thing about that place was that, fifty million billion squillion years into the future or however long it was, fashions seem to have regressed by twenty or so.

HILL, THE: John Levene recommends this Sean Connery film during his entertaining but ever-so-slightly bonkers DVD commentary[*] for 'Inferno', claiming that it's similar to the episodes under discussion. Be warned: This is a ruse designed to lure *Doctor Who* fans into watching something other than the BBC science-fiction show. While *The Hill* is indeed a great film, there is no sign of an eye-patch-wearing Sean digging to the Earth's crust in a parallel universe. We did spot Tony Caunter from 'The Crusade', 'Colony in Space' and 'Enlightenment', though.

---

[*] Recorded separately from the main one, we hear, to take advantage of a rare visit by John to the UK. It's all very well stockpiling these things – and 'The Keeper of Traken' will work, we suppose, as a tribute to Anthony Ainley – but surely, eventually, some of those longer-delayed commentaries are going to become less than topical. It only takes one remark along the lines of 'Ooh, wouldn't it be nice if *Doctor Who* came back'...

HIS AND HERS: In fairness to *Doctor Who Magazine*, it's not often in its long history that it's resorted to the cynical marketing ploy of publishing multiple covers for an issue. But their suggestion that having a David cover and a Billie cover to herald the start of Series Two was just giving fans the chance to pick their favourite character was a bit of a cheek. Really, it's akin to asking an alcoholic to choose between vodka and gin – they're going to want both, aren't they? Luckily, those of us determined to stick to just one single copy were aided in our choice by the decision to use a photo of Billie that made her look like Pete Burns off *Celebrity Big Brother*.

'HOORAY!': Exclamation with which Russell T greets just about any idea of his, or any mention of his show, or sometimes even just his own name in *Doctor Who* podcasts and commentaries.

HOW TO TELL IF THE SHADOWY FORM APPEARING AT REGULAR INTERVALS IS A CYBERNETIC CREATURE ATTEMPTING TO BREAK THROUGH FROM A PARALLEL UNIVERSE OR THE GHOSTLY MANIFESTATION OF A DECEASED LOVED ONE: You can't. Odd, that.

HYLAND, IAN: Whoever said there was no such thing as bad publicity probably never read Ian's TV review column in the *News of the World*. For his review of 'Rise of the Cybermen', he compared David Tennant to Dick Van Dyke in *Mary Poppins*, bemoaned the lack of chemistry between Tennant and Billie, commented on Roger Lloyd-Pack's overacting and said the Cybermen looked gay. Fortunately, he liked this one – it was his favourite episode so far.

'I WAS A DAD ONCE': Ha! Thought this'd get the fans all worked up, did you? You'll have to do much better than that, what with everyone knowing he's a grandfather and one thing leading to another and everything. The books have also given us Gallifreyan looms and an adopted daughter – so really, this is in no way conclusive proof of a bonking Doctor, and certainly not when weighed up against forty-three years of apparent abstinence. Our latest theory is this: that certain things can't be regenerated, and that the First Doctor used up all of his before we met him.

ICE WARRIORS: Mildly punny heading we planned to use for the *DANCING ON ICE* entry, but *DWM* beat us to it. The swines! But speaking of Ice Warriors, now that all the A-List monsters have been done, rumours are rife about this mob coming back for 2007. Russell T has denied it, and also denied a double bluff. But, perhaps significantly, he's never denied that his denial of a double bluff might be a triple bluff. Without the benefit of a TARDIS (except the money box one, which is admittedly great but not so much at time travel), we can only wait and see. We reckon it'll be them or the Sontarans, anyway. Or the Zygons.

'I'D LIKE TO BE VERY SILLY ON THIS FORUM': Question (sic) 1.1 of the FAQs for the Restoration Team's online forum. To which the answer is: 'This isn't the place to be silly, because we're very serious.' So, you've been told.

IDIOTS: Hey, we just realised 'idiot's lantern' is a term for telly... But we're always watching telly!

IMDB: We always wondered if actors read the posts on their own message boards here. Well, in 2004, a fan begged Sophia Myles to appear in the new *Doctor Who* and, lo and behold, in 2006 she's 'The Girl in the Fireplace' (would this be a good place for the 'poker' joke, or is it best just to leave it?). Wonder what else they'll do if you ask nicely? Hmm, 'Dear Miss Bryant...' See also **LOVETT, NORMAN**.

INFLATABLE DALEK*: Though one of these famously appeared with a victorious England Cricket team in 2006, emblazoned with the words 'Aussies Exterminated', we reckon the manufacturers missed a trick in not marketing blow-up models of Captain Jack and Rose instead. Not that we'd buy the former, of course. Or, ahem, even a Rose one actually, but given the choice...

INFORMATION TEXT: Useful and, erm, informative feature on the DVDs. For example you'll discover that associate producer Mervyn Pinfield invented the autocue – and doubtless lots of *Doctor Who* trivia too, we forget. Of course, Region 1 viewers will be better informed than us Brits about 'Vengeance on Varos', thanks to their text lasting until the end, but let's not be bitter. The most significant thing to be learned, however, is that you must always take what is said in the commentaries with a pinch of salt. They don't half make up some whoppers.

TEN More Things That Could Have Been Included as Extras on The Series 1 DVD Box Set

1. *A New Dimension* – documentary by the producers of *Doctor Who Confidential*, which aired on BBC One before 'Rose'.

2. *The Ultimate Guide* – documentary by the producers of *Doctor Who Confidential*, which aired on BBC One before 'The Parting

---

* Not to be confused with the 'inflatable Dalek' given away with *Doctor Who Adventures*, which was more accurately a balloon with a picture of a Dalek on it.

of the Ways'.

3. *Doctor Who Confidential* episode one.

4. *Doctor Who Confidential* episode two.

5. *Doctor Who Confidential* episode three.

6. *Doctor Who Confidential* episode four.

7. *Doctor Who Confidential* episode five.

8. *Doctor Who Confidential* episode six.

9. *Doctor Who Confidential* episode seven.

10. *Doctor Who Confidential* episodes eight to thirteen.

INSECTS: On a strange world where overgrown spiders spin deadly webs, our heroes face danger from giant ants, but help is at hand from a big butterfly. Ha ha, fooled you, no that isn't a rubbish description of 'The Web Planet' – at least not the *Doctor Who* one – it's a *Captain Scarlet* comic strip adventure from a 1968 issue of *TV21*. Wonder where that idea came from?

'INTER ME MATE': Another great *Sun* pun, when they learned that *Doctor Who* fan Tim Haws had been buried in a coffin shaped like a TARDIS (well, like half a TARDIS – he wasn't a big fat git or anything).

INTERACTIVE ELECTRONIC BOARD GAME, THE: Is there a more overused word than 'interactive' these days? We think not. In this case, it presumably refers to the big fat TARDIS model that sits at the centre of the latest bog-standard *Doctor Who* board game dispensing good or bad fortune at the touch of a button – obviously much more 'interactive' than the customary pile of cards! Meanwhile, multiple Ninth Doctors compete to gather components from such diverse old haunts as London, London and Cardiff. They also control a small army of Daleks, and can turn them against anyone who looks like winning – which, with four players or more, serves to prolong the jollity by many, many hours. We eventually gave up and let the Daleks win; it seemed only fair.

'INVASION, THE' – THE ANIMATED VERSION: Having Cosgrove Hall recreate the two missing episodes is undoubtedly a very interesting development in *Doctor Who* history. The Chorlton-based animation firm have performed sterling work recapturing the spirit of the sixties originals, which bodes well for similar projects in the future. The likenesses of the three protagonists are spot on and... Hang on, why is Zoe dressed like that in the TARDIS scenes? She should still be wearing her spangly silver catsuit from 'The Mind Robber'. OK, stop the cartoon right now – it's all gone pear-shaped!

'IT WAS SUPPOSED TO BE THE SIZE OF A DOUBLE-DECKER BUS': Classic quote from disappointed *Blue Peter* competition winner William Grantham, when his Abzorbaloff turned out to be only as big as Peter Kay (pretty big, even so). Russell T riposted that Grantham hadn't specified any such thing on his entry – and we're betting that, if he had, he'd never have seen his creation on the telly. So maybe he should just count his blessings. Although, looking at the winning design again, you have to wonder what Russell made of those tiny human heads – and, in one case, an entire body – protruding from the Abzorbaloff's flesh. Did he think it had absorbed a tribe of pygmies or what? It was also a bit disingenuous of Russell to have Rose remark on the monster's similarities to his own creations, the Slitheen (when the Abzorbaloff looked more like *Fungus the Bogeyman* anyway). Big and green the Abzorbaloff may have been, but we'd lay odds that the fart gag was not the work of young Master Grantham, who was, after all, nine years old.

TEN Marvellous Entrants in the *Blue Peter* Design-a-Monster Competition 2005

1. Sad Tony: Blubbering, 'elephant-y' creature that took second place in the seven and under age group. It isn't really called Sad Tony, of course, that would be silly – its real name is unpronounceable. Ha! Disguising the bland nature of your monster by giving it a really long name – that'll never work!

2. The Watcher: So called because it had lots of eyes and doubtless

not, as *BP* presenter Matt (or was it Gethin?) commented, because it had six arms and could wear loads of watches.

3. The Babster: An evil baby, which scratches, bites, sheds deadly tears and emits ear-piercing screams. Best of all: 'When the baby does the toilet, the smell causes the unfortunate nappy-changer to start dribbling uncontrollably and shrivel up like a raisen (sic).' So... a normal baby, then.

4. Vincent Veggie: A monster composed of broccoli and peas – which, from what we can gather, forces people to eat vegetables. Such evil can hardly be comprehended.

5. Mutated Caveman: Uses its massive ears to stun people, so a match-up against the Ninth Doctor would have been inevitable.

6. The Football Monster: Basically, some footballs stuck together. In bygone, budget-conscious days, this would surely have won the grand prize. Regardless, Russell T must have kicked himself when he realised that 'Love & Monsters' was airing at the height of World Cup fever. A missed opportunity.

7. The Horrible Herb: Cor, those kids really hate vegetable matter, don't they? Has Jamie Oliver achieved nothing? This scary creature 'would probably kill you if you ate it', which seems a somewhat counterproductive route to universal domination.

8. The Post Box: Yup, it's a post box come to life to destroy its enemies. No doubt with a comedy burp sound effect.

9. Scarecrows: Suggested by at least two entrants, one of whom gave his straw man a pumpkin head for extra fright value (pumpkins being, of course, universally acknowledged as the scariest things ever – well, they *are* vegetables). But hold on, competition rules stated that the monsters should be all-new and never have appeared in *Doctor Who* before. Have these people never heard of the 1969 *TV Comic* strip 'The Night Walkers'? What are they teaching them in schools these days? Did we fill *DWM* with pages of waffle about spin-off adventures in vain?

10. The *Blue Peter* Monster. With the heads of all the current *Blue Peter* presenters. We can just see it now, whipping out its space gun with a four-throated cry of 'Here's one I prepared earlier.'

'IT'S A NIGHTMARE. HER FLATULENCE IS A BIG PROBLEM': David Tennant on working with Billie Piper, as reported – apparently in all seriousness – by the *Manchester Evening News*. We suspect a journalistic sense of humour failure, as we can't believe anything bad could come out of that amazing bottom.

'IT'S NOT BEING MADE FOR US': The rallying cry of fans desperate not to hear a bad word said about any aspect of new *Doctor Who*, even if they agree with it. Why are you still watching it, then?

JABE: The Doctor gave her breath from his lungs. In return, she gave him wood.*

JACKET, LEATHER: All right, so the new series Doctor is more romantic hero than eccentric boffin – and we'd be the last people on Earth to advocate a return to the dark days of question mark jumpers and multi-coloured patchwork coats. But can't we at least have a costume that looks like a designer actually made it rather than just bought it off the peg at Matalan?

Aside from anything else, anything that makes a certain type of fan think it's suddenly acceptable to dress as their hero in public must be fiercely resisted. They might think they're clever, strutting about in their Salford street clobber or their geek chic suits, thinking no one will notice and laugh at them. But go to any *Doctor Who* event these days, and the sheer number of sweaty leather jackets on display makes it cringingly obvious.

JONES, HARRIET: Once the Prime Minister of... oh, you knew that, did you? Harriet was abducted by aliens but subsequently helped thwart their attempt to enslave half of humanity. A perfectly legitimate excuse for looking a bit tired, you'd think. More recently, she was seen handling standby props for 'Love & Monsters'. See also **GOLDEN AGE**.

---

* One for our American readers, this.

JONES, MARTHA: So, Rose was spared the pruning we feared, but her seasons are over and we can now look forward to seeing Freema Agyeman in full bloom instead (did you spot the floral motif going on there?). She's a pretty girl to be sure, but can she act? It's impossible to say yet, as it would be grossly unfair to assess anyone's ability based on their appearances in *Crossroads*. Freema's *Doctor Who* debut doesn't provide much of an indication either – what with Adeola meeting such a swift demise at the hands of, well, the Doctor actually, despite his feeble attempts to blame the Cybermen.

JUNIOR MASTERMIND: Tuning in to the final of this show to see Sam from Rutland answering questions on the Christopher Eccleston Months turned out to be a slightly humiliating experience due to the superior knowledge displayed by the youthful contestants. The little swots – why aren't they out binge drinking and having babies like normal kids? We take solace in the fact that Sam only had to study thirteen episodes for his appearance; ask him the story code of 'The Underwater Menace' and he wouldn't have been laughing, oh no! Sadly, he only achieved fifth place out of six – but at least he beat the Chelsea fan. And as some consolation, he got to meet a certain 'unemployed Timelord (sic)' from Salford...

JUSTICIA: The Doctor's visit to this penal colony in *The Monsters Inside* is mentioned in 'Boom Town' – which is surely the world's first example of a TV series canonising the events of its own tie-in books (though mentions of Lucifer and Arcadia in other episodes may have been sly New Adventures references). The only problem with this, and all those other alien worlds name checked by Rose, was that it made us wonder why we weren't *seeing* any of them, instead of bloody Cardiff again.

K1: The designation for the robot in 'Robot'. We knew that, honest! He was popular enough to appear on a Weetabix card and on a jigsaw puzzle with some of his giant robotic mates. And more recently original voice Michael Kilgarriff reprised the role in the Benny audio *Relics of Jegg-Sau*. Suppose that's another way to make them appeal to *Doctor Who* fans.

KALDOR CITY: It's tempting to suggest that, with Big Finish and BBV having nabbed all the interesting spin-off series, Magic Bullet Productions weren't left with much. But their audio range based on a single story, 'The Robots of Death', is quite interesting really, and could open up the way for more of the same.* Of particular note is Scott Fredericks' character Carnell, who first appeared, played by the same actor, in Chris Boucher's *Blake's 7* episode 'Weapon' and also turned up in the same author's PDA *Corpse Marker*. You'd think the first proper *Doctor Who/ Blake's 7* crossover would be a bit more exciting, wouldn't you? See also **WHO'S BLAKE**.

---

* Though, of course, this should only be attempted with stories that were actually popular. It would be madness to produce, say, an audio follow-up to 'Time and the Rani'. By the way, anyone got round to listening to *The Rani Reaps the Whirlwind* yet?

KAY, PETER*: Quick, send for Derek Acorah, the spirit of J John Nathan-Turner has possessed the casting director. See also **TATE, CATHERINE** (if we can be bothered to write the entry, that is).

KENNEDY, VICTOR: A Whizzkid for the twenty-first century. 'I don't like to be touched,' says Kennedy, 'literally or metaphorically' – in one fell swoop, a swipe at fans who've criticised the Welsh series' soapy elements, and an old-school dig at their imagined virginity. Unlike JNT, though, RTD shows the other side of the coin with LINDA: a group who, united by a shared interest in the Doctor, expand their horizons and enjoy full social – and sex – lives. (Oddly, though, they're all heterosexual – don't see **GAY AGENDA**.) That is, until a 'Super Fan' (Russell's description, from *DWM*) comes along to complain that they aren't taking their hobby seriously enough, and takes all the fun out of it for them. Kennedy's obsession is with the missing episodes of *Doctor Who*, hence lines like 'You'll never know what he was doing in your house all those years ago,' and his attempts to chart the Doctor's adventures using audio recordings where no pictures are available. Of course, the fact that he's also a big fat monster (see **'IT WAS SUPPOSED TO BE THE SIZE OF A DOUBLE-DECKER BUS'**) is where the comparisons with any particular 'Super Fan' must end. Though for some entertaining suggestions, see Ian Levine's Internet forum.

TEN Productions That Featured Fictional *Doctor Who* Fans

1. Not long after the original show was cancelled, the BBC showed just what they thought of disgruntled 'barkers' by introducing dim-witted Whovian Trevor Short into *EastEnders*.

2. Oliver Morris was a last-series replacement character in Steven Moffat's *Coupling* – a sitcom that already featured a Steven Taylor – and who accidentally wore a 'Bring Back *Doctor Who'* sweatshirt to a date, and dreamt of discussing the recovery of old episodes with an actual woman. The series didn't do a great deal to overthrow the sexless stereotype, describing Oliver's science-

---

* By the way, we felt a garlic bread-related pun substituting Dalek for garlic was far too obvious to deserve an entry of its own, so this footnote will have to suffice.

fiction bookshop as 'the Headquarters of Lonely' – but hey, he got to bonk Gina Bellman, so there's hope.

3. Back in 1991, the Verity Lambert-produced *GBH* took an outsiders' view, as Robert Lindsay's lead character found himself in a convention hotel surrounded by costumed loons.

4. Nor were any stereotypes overturned in Colin Sharpe's Radio 7 play *Dalek I Love You*, in which lead character Nigel's *Who* obsession seems to be the product of a mental illness. Still, despite believing he's the illegitimate son of Jon Pertwee, Nigel gets off with his very own Romana.

5. On the other hand, Radio 3's *Regenerations* by Daragh Carville (guest-starring Tom Baker and Sophie Aldred as themselves) is doubtless the most fair and truthful portrayal of fans to date, set at a Belfast convention and featuring some 'dorks', many gay men, a few people ashamed about the whole thing and some just there to get drunk. There's also a mention of Tom Baker underpants.

6. Fans of homosexuality were surely enraged by Russell T's obvious *Doctor Who* agenda in *Queer as Folk*. The character of Vince Tyler (some relation?) rarely missed the opportunity to show off a *Who* video or a model of K9, and there's that famous scene where he brings a bloke back to his flat to find 'Genesis of the Daleks' a greater attraction than sex. The favour was almost returned when, according to *QAF* star Anthony Cotton, he was asked to appear in the Welsh series as a 'gay-lien' (see **GAY AGENDA**). Sadly, he was too busy playing *Coronation Street*'s camp knicker-stitcher Sean Tully.

7. Alongside Yates and Benton and Franklin and Levene, *Recall UNIT* featured an evil (and, uniquely for this list, female) *Who* fan called Bergbo who was working with the Master – and a good fan called Tim who helped save the world. Nope, still don't understand a word of it.

8. In 1995, future Big Finish writer Nev Fountain penned a semi-autobiographical play, 'My Grandmother was a Time Lord', in which marketing executive Ian Foreman met his younger, scarf-wearing fanatical eight year-old self. And other than that, we know nowt about it.

9. Extinct C4 soap *Brookside* once boasted no fewer than two fans among its cast – and both were normal, well-adjusted people with girlfriends and everything. Doctor Darren Roebuck shared a *Friends*-inspired tempestuous relationship with Victoria Wilcox, whom he once dragged to a convention and alongside whom he left the series. Clint Moffat, whose girlfriend Katie Rogers once bought him a World Distributors annual, had a more typical *Brookie* departure, being accidentally killed by another regular.

10. And finally, there are no definite fan sightings yet in the grandmother of British soaps – but, one Sunday evening in May 2005, we glimpsed *Doctor Who Magazine* on a shelf in *Coronation Street*'s Kabin – and it wasn't there next time we looked. Who could have bought it? Could Ken Barlow have slipped it into the pages of his *Independent*? Could Eileen Grimshaw have been looking for news of her absentee son? Was Janice Battersby desperate for Archive features on... oh, let's face it, it was Sean Tully, wasn't it!

'KINDA' SURPRISE: So, it turns out Christopher Bailey is a real person after all, and *DWM* tracked him down for an interview and everything. Not that most of us thought otherwise – but at least it puts paid to the widely-believed rumours (among mentalist fans, that is) that 'Kinda' was in fact written by sexy songstress Kate Bush using a pseudonym. No idea who really wrote 'Snakedance', though; Jay Aston out of Bucks Fizz, probably.

KING RALPH: Movie in which an American finds himself next in line to the British throne (yeah, right – we'd become a republic first!). Anyway, it's worth a look for the very lovely Camille Coduri dancing about the place in a skimpy showgirl outfit.

KOOKABURRA SONG, THE: As recited in 'Fear Her', a charming children's ditty that culminates in the line 'Gay your life must be'. So, it's subliminal commands to the nation's youth now, is it! See **GAY AGENDA**.

KRILLITANES: Originally Krillians, their name was changed to avoid an alleged trademark clash (we carried out extensive research – well, Googled – but we're none the wiser really) – a fact that someone might have told Character Options before they announced their action figure.

The *DWM* letters page beat us to the observation that their ugly mugs bear a striking resemblance to the Malevilus – but still, any excuse to mention *The Iron Legion* again, recently given a long-awaited fifth airing as a trade paperback. How about a 3-D version in *Doctor Who Adventures* next? They could give away glasses like what the Tenth Doctor wears. Or maybe they could serialise it across the backs of chocolate wrappers? Though we'd probably just end up missing the last one...

LARDIS: *DWM*'s nickname for the big fat shed-like TARDIS when it was first unveiled – and probably the most, and last, critical thing they ever said about the Welsh series. Dunno what the L is supposed to stand for, though – London, probably.

LAWLESS, LUCY*: A spoof website made a spoof claim – which, from the outset, they admitted was a spoof – that Lucy Lawless was to replace David Tennant as the Doctor in Series Three. Yet, although it even sounded like a spoof (because it was indeed a spoof), it was reported in some quarters as a piece of news and not a spoof. So in case you were fooled and are expecting Ms Lawless to appear at the helm of the TARDIS next year, it won't be happening after all because, all together now, it was ... bullsh*t.

LAZENBY, GEORGE: One-shot James Bond actor, constantly compared to Paul McGann by fans and journalists desperate to eke out their theory of 'uncanny' *Who*/ Bond parallels (see **BOND, JAMES BOND** in Volume 1). Stretching this analogy even further beyond breaking point, they also claim that Christopher Eccleston is *Doctor Who*'s Tim Dalton. Hmm. Not completely accurate, we reckon. Colin Baker should be Dalton, as the rug was pulled out from under him too soon – whereas Eccleston should be Lazenby as he left after one attempt. As for McGann... well, he's Barry Nelson, of course.

---

* Still, any excuse to mention her, really.

LE DOCTEUR OMEGA: Elderly, white-haired space traveller who flew to Mars in his home-made ship *Cosmos* in 1906, under the guiding pen of French author Arnould Galopin. Much has been made of this Doctor Omega's similarities to our own First Doctor – particularly by Black Coat Press, who hoped to flog an English translation of Galopin's work to fans. Unfortunately, they rather muddied the issue by inserting new references to *Doctor Who* continuity willy-nilly. Were Susan and the Ice Warriors really part of the novelist's original vision? Somehow, we doubt it. Still, as Black Coat insist on pointing out, the Greek letter omega is used to represent the ohm, a unit of electrical resistance – and when you spell OHM in capital letters and turn it upside down, you get... WHO!! Well, that's us convinced.

TEN Fictional Characters Who Aren't The Doctor, No Honest They Aren't

1. The Stranger (various videos and audios). Played by Colin Baker and accompanied for his first few adventures by Nicola Bryant as Miss Brown (no relation). Somehow, we think we might be hearing more of producers BBV by the time this list's done.

2. The Dentist (*Shakedown*). Ah, but wait – when this Reeltime Productions film made an unexpected bid for canonicity, by being turned into a New Adventure with the Doctor in it and everything, it suddenly turned out that the Dentist was the Doctor all along. Who'da thought it?

3. The Professor/ the Dominie (various audios). Yup, BBV again. This time, it's Sylvester McCoy and Sophie Aldred who play the Professor and Ace (no relation). At least they did, until the BBC raised a stern eyebrow and a swift re-branding exercise was required. The characters returned as the completely dissimilar Dominie and Alice.

4. The Wanderer (various audios). This time, BBV didn't even fork out for a Doctor from the telly, though they got the next best thing: Dalek voice Nicholas Briggs, also known for his acclaimed

run as the Doctor in the unofficial Audio Visuals releases of yonks back, and of course as the face of *DWM*'s oh-no-he-isn't-really comic strip Ninth Doctor. They even crossed him over with their Cyberon line, not at all based on the Cybermen (nor, we assume, on the Cyberons from the *Space: 1999* comic strip in *Look-In*).

5. Doctor Diamond. Another frock-coated, time-travelling adventurer; this one had a Time Clock, and hung out with *Kelly's Eye* (and no doubt the rest of Kelly too) in the pages of the *Valiant* comic.

6. Aztec Ace (Eclipse comic book series). In 1984, Doug Moench's sixteenth-century time traveller fought to save future history from his arch-enemy Nine-Crocodile. Actually, looking at this again, it's a bit unfair to dismiss Ace (no relation) as a Doctor wannabe – but we need to fill the list up so, erm, how about Marvel's Professor Gamble? See **DREDLOX, THE** in Volume 1.

7. The Chief Physician (*X-Men: The Chaos Engine Trilogy*). Marvel tie-in novels by *Short Trips* author Steve Roman, set partly in Merlin's Otherworld of the *Captain Britain* strips. A mysterious medic who looks like the Seventh Doctor appears, disappears, and returns in a guise not dissimilar to that of the Fourth. Fair enough, as Merlin himself had already crossed over into that universe from the *DWM* strip.

8. The Foot Doctor/Chiropodist (*Do You Have a Licence to Save This Planet?*). Oi, this isn't fair – BBV taking the rip out of themselves before we can!

9. Doctor Poo (*Viz*). One-off comic strip character who travelled space and time in search of a lavatory. There's actually nothing in the strip to suggest this isn't the bona fide Doctor, albeit travelling in his fourth incarnation with Jamie. His attempts to drop his load are interrupted by Davros, the Daleks, the Cybermen, the Master and the Sea Devils, so presumably a hefty legal bill there if the wrong people notice.

10. Doctor Nick Cutter (*Primaeval*). Nah, just our little joke.

LESLIE, JOHN: Apparently (it was in *The Sun* so must be true) he was very keen to land the role of the Tenth Doctor. Punch line removed for legal reasons.

LISTED PROGRAMMES: So you see, Michael Grade, you didn't need to suspend or cancel *Doctor Who*, and thus deprive a generation or two of British children of what should have been their birthright, did you? You just needed to put the right people on the job, and hey presto, as popular as ever. Eat humble pie, you sod!

To prevent such short-sightedness in the future, we suggest *Doctor Who* be granted 'listed' status just as British buildings of great architectural merit are to protect them from unsympathetic development or bulldozing in favour of housing. That way, even if no one watched it like in the eighties, the show couldn't be cancelled. This would also apply to other culturally important series, preserving *Coronation Street*, *Blue Peter* and *Grange Hill* (but not *Last of the Summer Wine*) for future generations whether they want to watch them or not. We've already lost *Top of the Pops*, *Grandstand* and *The Sooty Show* – action must be taken!

LITTLE RED RIDING HOOD: Fairy tale that may or may not have been an influence on the Bad Wolf story arc. Certainly, when we first see Rose she's wearing a red hood – well, a reddish hoodie. And Jack the woodcutter could well have been reincarnated as Captain Jack. Or Jackie. And what big ears that Ninth Doctor had! The little pig, granted, does come from an entirely different 'bad wolf' story – but note how Little Red was eventually consumed by her wolf, only to be implausibly resurrected by a Deus Ex Machina ending. The jury's still out.

LONDON MARATHON 2006: A Black Dalek took part in this race, but as none of the other competitors were exterminated it was most likely a human being in an elaborate costume. Other weird creatures taking part included Chewbacca, a dragon and Jade Goody out of *Big Brother*.

LOOK WHAT THIS TWATT'S BUILT: Number #1 rule for dealing with the tabloid press as a *Doctor Who* fan: If your surname lends itself to any sort of pun... don't. But then, the *Daily Star* seemed out to get artist Raymond Twatt from the start, describing his homemade Dalek as a 'load of ballcocks' (because he used some ballcocks in its construction, geddit?) and a 'loo-ny idea'. 'Some of the neighbours probably think I'm a bit mad,' said Twatt, giving the paper the ideal excuse to use the subheading 'Mad'. Raymond has since changed his name.

LOONEY TUNES BACK IN ACTION: Magnificent Bugs Bunny-starring part-animation, part-live action movie. To Tim Hancock's frustration, it boasted an appearance by the Daleks, locked up in a desert research base alongside the Metaluna mutant and a bunch of other classic movie aliens. Clearly, then, another BBC attempt at brand ruination – though, as far as we can tell, this one must have been set in motion four decades earlier when the Cushing movies were licensed. Hmm, does that mean Warner Brothers have the rights to use the Daleks in perpetuity? Could they turn up fighting Batman or Detective Chimp in a DC comic? Answers on a postcard, please. In the meantime, we're just happy with the proof that at least one version of the Daleks exists in the same universe as Scooby-Doo. Zoinks!

'LOVE & MONSTERS': A work of genius or a right pile of old sh*t, nobody is sure. Either way, Russell T is to be commended for taking *Doctor Who*'s elastic format to the point where it's in danger of getting stretch marks – even if he was channelling that *Buffy* episode where Andrew the Geek makes a video diary when he wrote it.

LOVETT, NORMAN: Comedian and *Red Dwarf* actor rumoured to be appearing as Davros in 'The Parting of the Ways'. Well, not so much a rumour as an outright lie. Which is the problem with the Internet Movie Data Base and its policy of letting just anyone alter its entries (see also Wikipedia). More lies added to the IMDB's 'Doomsday' listing included Terry Molloy reclaiming his role as the Daleks' creator and the return of Captain Jack for Series Two, so presumably someone still thinks this sort of thing is funny. That's not a joke, though, that's just being a tosser.

LUMIC, JOHN: As crippled, evil masterminds behind the creation of iconic *Doctor Who* monsters go he's OK, but he's no Davros.

LUMLEY, JOANNA: Well, we did say the only excuse for a female Doctor was that Joanna Lumley could play her – and to date, neither 'The Curse of Fatal Death' nor 'Exile' have challenged that view. Yes, how delighted we were when the lovely Joanna brought her Dalek bumps to bear on Jonathan Pryce's Master. But of course, it caused uproar among fans – because, frankly, what doesn't? Joanna was the thirteenth Doctor, went the whinge, so obviously the BBC were burning up those final regenerations to avoid bringing the show back. Yeah, cos they've always included Doctors from comedy sketches when they're counting, haven't they! (See also **QUITTER, THE.**) Though come to think of it, despite the jokes and the comedy breasts, 'tCoFD' was a lot less ridiculous than 'Dimensions in Time', the Doctor had the least rubbish costume since the seventies and it came out on video in the same format as the series, so we can see the confusion.

MANCHESTER SUITE: At last! After forty-two years, the first ever mention of Manchester in TV *Doctor Who* – and it only took 'The End of the World' to bring it about.

MASSIVE SOD: Maybe it's cos Terrance Dicks only wrote one Target book for the Sixth Doctor, but we've never had a pithy description of the him to match, say, 'cosmic hobo' or 'wide-eyed Bohemian'. That is, until the *Guardian's* preview of 'Rose', which offered this perfect suggestion (though it also claimed the Autons were ripped off from an eighties Kraftwerk video, so minus several hundred points for that). We're offering a grand prize of one shiny English pound to the first person who can work this lovely phrase into a licensed piece of *Doctor Who* fiction. Two pounds if you can get the Fourth Doctor to say: 'So you're my replacements – an open-faced young man and a massive sod.' And no, sending it via BT Text doesn't count.

McDONALD WITHOUT AN A: Did you know that David Tennant hasn't always gone by that name? He used to be Neil Tennant out of the Pet Shop Boys! Or was he the other one? Anyway, something like that, we forget the actual anecdote... We just assumed he'd named himself after the lager.

McGANNISTS: Whovian subculture dedicated to restoring Paul McGann to his former role in *Doctor Who* whether he wants to return or not. First, this small but delusional band campaigned for him to be in the first Welsh series – and you'd have thought Chris Eccleston's casting would have put 'em off, but not a bit of it. As soon as his departure was announced, they were back on the forums like rats up drainpipes, with suggestions for Paul's miraculous return. Don't even get us started on the Bring Back Peter Davison campaign! Anyway, for reasons explained under *GROUND ZERO*, surely there are more than enough Eighth Doctor stories out there already...?

TEN Non-TV Companions to The Eighth Doctor

1. Bernice Summerfield. Virgin saw out their line of New Adventures by having Benny jump the Doctor's bones. Typical!

2. Izzy, from the *DWM* comic strip, who came out of the closet before Russell T's gay agenda (not that there is one) had even been drawn up.

3. Ramsay the Vortisaur. Hooray, a dinosaur in the TARDIS! Why couldn't he have stayed?

4. Ssard, an Ice Warrior from the *Radio Times* comic strip, which presumably limited the places the Doctor could visit to nice cold ones.

5. Destrii, fish-faced comic strip companion who got into Izzy's body and vice versa. Though not in the way you're thinking, stop that at once.

6. Fitz Kreiner, sixties florist who – let's see if we've got this straight – was abandoned by the Doctor, kept in stasis for centuries, then corrupted into becoming a Faction Paradox agent and eventually flung into the Time Vortex for all eternity.

7. Fitz Kreiner nee Kode, a clone who conveniently replaced the above. So, that's all right, then.

8. Charley Pollard, pre-eminent Big Finish companion and

Edwardian adventuress who, when we first met her, was carrying on the grand tradition of girl *Doctor Who* companions in historical stories by being mistaken for a boy.

9. Compassion. EDA sidekick who improbably metamorphosed into a TARDIS and thus allowed the Eighth Doctor and Fitz to enter her, take her up the Milky Way, fiddle with her knobs, ride her to Heaven and back, etc., etc.

10. Um... Fey Truscott-Sade, Sam Jones (and so-called 'Dark Sam'), Anji Kapoor, Trix MacMillan, Stacey Townsend, Lucie Miller, C'rizz, Samson and Gemma Griffin... have we missed any? Y'see, this is why we feel forced to take the purist route and accept TV continuity only. So, basically what happened is that the Eighth Doctor went to a party, had a bit of a snog, then buggered off never to be seen again.

MIGHTY BOOSH, THE: Who'd have thought Vince Noir and Howard Moon's deadly encounter with the Betamax Bandit in this surreal BBC Three sitcom would foreshadow the Doctor's equally implausible battle with the Wire? Speaking of whom – funny how those fifties TV viewers wound up looking just like the blank-faced photograph man from *Sapphire & Steel*, but at least there was some kind of logic to his appearance. We suspect that, in real life, having your face sucked off would actually cause you to fall over and die. See also **WIRE, THE.**

'MILD INTEREST': Emotion with which attendees were asked to react to the appearance of a giant praying mantis in their midst at the 2000 Panopticon convention. Not that a real giant praying mantis had appeared, of course, it was just Big Finish getting themselves some cheap crowd effects for 'The Shadow of the Scourge'. Such deliberate restraint might seem strange to our American readers, as indeed it did to our editor (who was present at the time) – but we feel bound to point out that, as praying mantises, giant or otherwise, are not indigenous to the UK, we've never quite shared our US cousins' fascination with them as objects of terror. It's not like they're pumpkins with scary faces carved into them or anything!

In fact, we're really quite fond of these insects' appearances in all those old B-movies and comics, with their silly spindly bodies and their not-at-all scary ability to produce a high-pitched sound by rubbing their back legs together, and we were delighted when 'Scourge' finally afforded them some much-deserved recognition in this country. Having said that, if a giant praying mantis did indeed turn up at a *Doctor Who* convention one day, we'd probably be the first ones out the door while everyone else was still being mildly interested. You can't be too careful.

MIND YOUR LANGUAGE: ITV sitcom from an age when the genre wasn't shackled by political correctness. There was a *Doctor Who* joke in one episode: language teacher Barry Evans asked his foreign students if they knew about dialects and one of them replied that he knew 'Doctor Who and the Dialects'. Come to think of it, that's about as funny as the show got – but the Dialects, they could be used in one of those surreptitious Daleks-by-another-name porn films couldn't they? With lots of jokes about alien tongues.

MINISTRY OF MAYHEM: We knew that bitchy trampoline lady Cassandra must have made an impression upon her debut, when a makeshift, non-CGI version of her turned up on the following week's edition of this ITV kids' show. Maybe it was at this juncture that Russell T realised he'd been a little hasty by having her explode in a bloody mess, and began to plan her return. But take note, Russell, no one ever made a Slitheen on any children's shows.

MISTRESS, THE: Sadly not a whip-wielding, spike-heeled, leather-clad dominatrix (although we don't actually know what Lalla Ward wore for the recording), but a thinly-disguised – bordering on transparent really – Romana-like character in BBV's short-lived K9 audios. Come to think of it, though, why *isn't* there a proper Time Lady called the Mistress? Why isn't that the name of Kate O'Mara's character? See also **DOCTOR SCREW**.

MONDAS: Not only did this planet have a north, but – according to *Spare Parts* – it didn't have much else. Presumably it's because the (original) Cybermen are all northerners that they're so feckin' hard. Though we might also suggest that at least now we know where the Cybermats came from: upgraded whippets!

MONGS: Gah! How could we have missed 'War on Aquatica' out of our list of classic World stories last time out? How could we have left it to Gary Gillatt to point out, in his brilliant *From A to Z*, that the Doctor once encountered alien mongeese? And luminous dolphins called, er, Lumidolphs. You must be thinking that, far from being connoisseurs of the annuals, we just skim-read the bloody things like everyone else did. Well, it's not true. Well, not much. Cor, this must be how David Saunders felt when 'Castrovalva' somehow slipped out of his *Doctor Who* encyclopedia. In fact, there's an idea: With just a pair of scissors, some glue and a spare copy of this book (still available at a reasonable price from Mad Norwegian Press)...

'MONTE CARLO OR BUST': At last, a *Doctor Who* character – in Big Finish freebie 'The Veiled Leopard' to be precise – notices what's been staring them in the face for two decades: that Peri has big breasts. It was OK when they were on TV – no comment was needed – but if the best thing about the old series' leap to books and audios is that you don't have to look at the Sixth Doctor's costume, then the downside is that you can't see Peri's personality at all. When Erimem says 'In these dresses, it's definitely bust' and Peri muses 'Boob jokes now,' it's like the characters spring to life. We suggest, in future, a few background extras per story to shout 'Get 'em out' and 'Phwoaaaar' and the like. Or just an appropriate boingy sound effect during running scenes.

MOORE, MRS: Or whatever she was really called. Ooh, what a great idea of the Doctor's: her family think she's dead, but go and tell them she wasn't really, but she is now. That'll cheer 'em up.

MORGAN, RHODRI: First Minister of Wales, who, as gleefully reported in all newspapers, turned up at the BBC studios in Cardiff for a political interview, was mistaken for a *Doctor Who* extra and sent to be made up as a tree person. Cue jokes about grass roots politics, branching out into acting, feeling a bit of a sap, etc, etc. Or, if you're a *Daily Star* journalist imagining a love triangle between the Doctor, Rose and Jabe: 'No, I Don't Fancy a Tree-Some!'

MOXX OF BALHOON: Bastard offspring of the Mekon and the Grinch. Everyone seems to think his name is a gay innuendo of some kind, but no one's been able to prove it. See **GAY AGENDA**, maybe.

TEN   Unsung Monsters

1. The Mechonoids. Deadly and powerful rivals to the Daleks, with just one drawback: while the grating, metallic voices of the Daleks enhanced their evil alien presence, the Mechonoids had theirs provided by Larry the Lamb. Consequently, they failed to return for a second TV outing – though they did turn up in plen-

ty of spin-off products: comics, toys, annuals, a mini-album –
and, four decades later, a Big Finish audio. Hmm. Given Larry's
involvement, maybe these last two weren't the best vehicles to
boost their flagging career.

2. The Bandrils. We've only seen one of these reptilian glove pup-
pets, on a screen in 'Timelash'. Presumably, if they were to enjoy
an expanded role, they'd have to do most of their plotting from
behind a desk with 'Daemons' star Matthew Corbett as their
underling-cum-interpreter. 'What's that, you've tidied your
room and now you want to take over this wretched world? Well,
OK then, if you're sure all your toys are put away. All together
now: Izzy, wizzy, let's get busy...'

3. The Bio-Mechanoid. Or, as most of us know it, that monster
from 'Dragonfire'. This guy was up against it from the start.
There was everyone expecting some great fire-breathing dragon,
and up pops a reject from *Alien*. Obviously you don't get Sean
Connery on *Doctor Who*'s budget, but there's no excuse for mis-
leading us like that. This monster did finally live up to at least
one part of its story's title, however, when it burnt to a crisp in
the Longleat Exhibition blaze.

4. The Sensorites. If you think of them as the show's first post-
modern, ironic creations, they make perfect sense. Not only are
we treated to Susan's impression of one of them running (and
what other *Doctor Who* monster could stand up to that test?),
but the Sensorites themselves suddenly realise that they all look
the same.

5. The Plasmatons. Surely not even the saddest, most obsessive
fanboy who thought the telemovie was up to much could be
suffering from the delusion that 'Time-Flight' was any good. It's
possible, therefore, that, had they appeared in a better story, the
Plasmatons might have garnered a little more respect. After all,
look at the reputation the cuddly and furry Yeti acquired after
'The Web of Fear'.

6. The Gell Guards. Likewise, the Gell Guards had the misfortune
to appear in the tenth anniversary story, and were thus over-
shadowed by nostalgia-inducing appearances of earlier Doctors.
Had they not faced such stiff competition... oh, all right, we're
just making excuses.

7. Pink Terileptils. It's evident from 'The Visitation' that the Terileptils are a multi-racial society – what with the green one, the blue one and the one with red and black bits – so it shouldn't have been a surprise when that pink one turned up in 'Mindwarp'. As this Terileptil was clothed from head to claw, we can only assume that the ones in 'The Visitation' had abandoned their apparel and were going around buck naked. Maybe they weren't even hardened criminals after all, and had been sent to the tinclavic mines for indecent exposure (though, without a detailed knowledge of Terileptil physiology, who's to say this doesn't count as being a hardened criminal?).

8. The Fish People. No, don't laugh. It's more than likely that, if some real-life mad scientist took it upon himself to engineer scaly, aquatic hybrid humans, they'd look just like the ones in 'The Underwater Menace', if not even sillier.

9. The Rills. No wonder these guys get overlooked. Not only did the BBC wipe their only story, they apparently took only one photo of them, made just one copy of it and then let someone walk off with the thing. The picture turned up a while ago, so now we know just how scary they really are.

10. The Myrka. Forget all that arty-farty foreign rubbish like the opera and the ballet, pantomime is uniquely British and should therefore be cherished. In 'Warriors of the Deep', we were fortunate to witness a virtuoso performance from the two blokes out of *Rentaghost*, complemented by appropriate lighting and set design, not to mention that costume. Makes you proud to be a fan.

'MR WATSON, COME HERE, I WANT TO SEE YOU': Words spoken by Alexander Graham Bell during the first ever telephone call on 10 March 1876. Just in case you may have heard different.

MUIR, LYNSEY: Third assistant director who thought it would help her get her picture in the *Radio Times*' *Who Watch* if she was photographed having her bottom fondled by a Dalek. Her ambition was achieved. However in so doing, she may have risked the ire of the Nation Estate, who now pay close attention to where Daleks stick their plungers.

MUSEUM: Hooray, the *Doctor Who* Exhibition is back in Blackpool. Boo, it's not in the old location. Hooray, it's in a bigger venue. They're half-heartedly calling it a museum now, presumably to distinguish it from the exhibition at Brighton, erm, Leicester, no Cardiff... Liverpool; the one that got all the new series stuff, anyway. But if they're going to get pretentious, it's as well they're no longer using the dyslexic chimp that composed the original information signs for the exhibits. But really, sod the new series props and costumes, they'll turn up in due course. In the meantime, the Exhibition, sorry, Museum would be greatly improved by the inclusion of some cheap badges, pencils and publicity postcards in the shop – just like the old days.

MUSIC: That Murray Gold's music can be quite loud at times, can't it? ...WE SAID IT'S VERY LOUD, MURRAY GOLD'S MUSIC! Whenever we do something bordering on the fanatically geeky – like buying a sur-plus-to-requirements copy of *The Collected Ninth Doctor Comic Strips* just to maintain a complete run of *DWM* Special Editions – we put it into perspective by thinking of the poor saps who went to the trouble of attempting to burn CDs of Mr Gold's music by isolating the tracks from the 5.1 soundtrack on the DVDs. It's just as well that, at time of writing, the BBC are finally about to put them out of their misery (by releasing proper albums of the stuff, we mean, not by trapping them and killing them or anything).

MY PARTNER IS A SCI-FI FANATIC: Burning issue addressed by the *Kilroy* programme in July 1999. 'How would you like,' asked orange, Arab-hating presenter Kilroy-Silk, pointing to a 'Moonbase' Cyberman in the audience, 'to live with a man who dresses like that?' One poor fan was then ridiculed for wanting to record stuff off the telly and, shock horror, *edit out the adverts* – while one particularly sanctimonious couple complained that it's wrong to watch science-fiction when you could be out helping children in Kosovo instead (not that they'd ever done so themselves).

Then we got to the nub of the issue, as the 'long-suffering' partners in the audience agreed it would be worse to be married to football fans. As unhappy as Kilroy was with that sentiment, he actually fled from the guy who pointed out that more people are more obsessive about religion, and isn't that just good science-fiction anyway? Such sentiments, the presenter feared, might land his show in trouble...

MYERS, STUART: His autograph appears on a Strictly Ink Doctor Who Series Two Trading Card (# AU-3, if you feel compelled to go out and collect it), which depicts a couple of Cybermen from different eras. OK, feel free to call us ignorant – but who is he?*

MYLES, SOPHIA: It seems she and David Tennant got on rather well when she guest-starred in 'The Girl in the Fireplace' – and although we're not usually bothered in the slightest about what actors get up to in their private lives, we found it amusing that Doctor Who was dating Lady Penelope. Imagine if the equivalent relationship had occurred in the mid-sixties – it would have been so wrong on so many levels.

MYRKA: Well, someone must have liked it – because not only did Big Finish bring it back in 'Bloodtide', but its debut TV story was turned into a talking book and now we hear there's a soundtrack release on its way. Perhaps the hope is that, given enough audio outings, we'll forget what it actually looked like and hail it as one of the scariest-sounding monsters of the twentieth century.

MYSTERY CHARACTER: For the benefit of those too stingy to send off 10p to get the completion certificate sticker for the Merlin album, it was the CyberController. See **STICKER ALBUM (AND STICKERS TO GO IN IT).**

---

* And why, when you scroll over the card's image on the Strictly Ink site, does it say 'Wendy'? Hmm, a case of a last-minute replacement there, we wonder? Though, knowing nothing about Stuart as we do, who's to say Wendy isn't his real name?

NAKED GIRL: It was quite rude of those Victorian soldiers to insult Rose's perfectly respectable attire. She ought to have retaliated by showing them just what a naked girl really does look like!

TEN Potential Titles for Anyone Thinking of Making More *Doctor Who* Porn (One for Each Doctor)

1. *Galaxy Foursome.* On a world of female clones, the First Doctor and Steven are given the pick of four hundred Dawns.

2. *The Whore Games.*

3. *The Curves of Peladon.* The Third Doctor faces some stiff opposition from Alpha Centauri.

4. *Genitals of the Daleks.* Hmm, better make that *Genitals of the Filthy F**king Phaleks,* to be on the safe side.

5. *Warriors of the Deep... Throat.*

6. *The Ultimate Blow.* The Sixth Doctor fends off the Vervoids with the only weapon to hand.

7. *The Hardpenis Patrol.* On the planet Terra Alpha, anyone not in a permanent state of arousal can expect a visit from the Randyman.

8. *Doctor Who – The Porn Movie.* Well, c'mon, we didn't have many Eighth Doctor titles to work with, did we?

9. *The Parting of the Legs.* Those kisses lead to something more.

10. *Nude Earth.* We could go on like this for pages, but no doubt you can come up with your own (and probably more disgusting) ideas by now.

NAME TAGS: Proudly worn on the heads of all new-series Daleks, and about time too, as this sensible suggestion was first made way back in the sixties, in the Souvenir Press Dalek books. How else are they meant to tell each other apart, after all?

NATIONAL HEALTH SERVICE: Here's a handy tip for Primary Care Trusts massively over budget and with increasing patient waiting lists. Simply take all the drugs out of the medicine cabinet, mix them up in a big bucket, pour the contents over the sick people, *et voila*, instant cure! Warning: this technique might not work as well as in 'New Earth', but worth a try surely?

NATIONAL TELEVISION AWARDS 2005: *Doctor Who* garnered three awards, including beating off stiff opposition like *The Bill* to land Best Drama – and, wearing a pleasingly short skirt, Billie picked up a solo gong, which turned out to be just one of many such accolades. Acting is obviously in her blood, which begs the question – what was that pop music career about? Oh, but hold on... *EastEnders* beating *Coronation Street* in the Best Soap category? So, once again, you can't take these things at all seriously.

'NEW EARTH': Among other things, Russell T wrote this one with animal testing in mind. Though he's been quoted as saying, 'Frankly, I don't say that I'm against animal testing at all, because I wouldn't look so beautiful without it.' So there you go, then: proof that testing cosmetics on animals is indeed a pointless waste of time.

'NEXT TIME...': Or 'Throw Forwards', as we're now supposed to call these sequences. Yet one more modern product of TV executives terrified that their actual programmes aren't good enough to keep viewers from turning over. Still, we suppose it wouldn't do to subject the kids to too much worry – these days, they'd probably sue – so it makes sense that, after every cliffhanger in new *Doctor Who*, we're now reassured of our heroes' ultimate safety. 'Aliens of London' was the first and worst offender; at least, for later two-parters, they had the sense to switch the clips to *after* the end titles. Or, in the case of 'Rise of the Cybermen', to do without them altogether and let the cliffhanger speak for itself. Hmmm, that seemed to work OK. Wonder why they didn't think of it before?

NIGHT OUT WITH PAUL CORNELL AND STEVEN MOFFAT, A: Holy crap, the things you stumble across while looking for Nestlés wrappers on eBay. It's all in a good cause (Crohn's disease), and they're smashing blokes and everything, but we're not sure it's worth the two and a half thousand dollar winning bid – they are both married men, after all. Come into the Waterhouse (the pub, not Matthew) in Manchester and you can have an evening with us for the price of a few pints. No funny business, though.

NORTON, GRAHAM: It's a good thing we don't believe in conspiracies, or it could have seemed that someone at the BBC was still out to get *Doctor Who*. The show's first proper episode in sixteen years, and they can't even press the right button to turn off the audio link to the *Strictly Come Dancing* studio! And so, the backstage chatter of camp presenter Graham Norton provided a surprise commentary track to Rose's first encounter with the Autons. Though, sadly for all those fans who must have pristine copies of each episode as originally broadcast, Graham's contribution was cut for the DVD release and didn't even feature as a deleted scene (but then, what did?).

NOT AMUSED: Queen Samantha... erm, Victoria ostensibly banished the Doctor and Rose from her world because they dabbled in magical stuff. But she'd earlier expressed an interest in the supernatural herself – and the Doctor had just saved her from a cartoon werewolf, so a bit hypocritical, surely? We reckon she just wanted rid of the pair of them for being smug and annoying.

OFFICER & CARS RESPOND TO ALL CALLS: Only one officer in charge of multiple cars? Tsk. That's police cutbacks for you.

'OH DEAR': Quiz master John Humphrys' much-trailered comment on *Doctor Who*'s becoming a *Mastermind* subject in 2004. Perhaps he'd forgotten that the first fan to answer questions on the good Doctor – Gavin Fuller* – had gone on to become the series' youngest ever champion in 1993. Nevertheless, Humphrys was on sparkling form, wittily pointing out that Daleks can't climb stairs, only to be corrected.

And there were no 'Oh dear's a year later when *Mastermind* jumped onto the back of the Welsh series with a special tie-in edition. Though maybe there ought to have been, as it was the contestant who scored lowest on *Who* itself who won, her general knowledge carrying her through. A lesson for us all there. Hilariously, John Humphrys joshed that Daleks can't climb stairs, only to be corrected. Alzheimer's, do you think? And why was the prize bowl emblazoned with the old logo? Perhaps they were worried that the winner might have thrown it to the floor in disgust if they'd used the new one. See also *JUNIOR MASTER-MIND*.

'OH MY GOD, I'M A CHAV!': OK, nitpicking time again. A very amusing line and all that – but why the expression of surprise from Cassandra?

---

* Fuller's specialist subject in the first round was *Doctor Who*; for the second, he narrowed it down to just 'The Crusades'. Is that allowed?

It's not as if she'd leapt into Rose's body at random: she'd seen her from the outside, and knew exactly who and what she was getting herself into. And the amusement ended completely when the whole thing turned out to be a cue for some 'Time and the Rani'-style impressions. Once again, we can't help thinking that John Nathan-Turner would have been burned in effigy outside the Fitzroy Tavern...

OKENODO, SOPHIE: Wasted as a cartoon. If she's not too busy in Hollywood making sh*te like *Aeon Flux*, maybe she could make a live action appearance as Alison Cheney in the Welsh series. And since they're unlikely to be needed for a sequel, perhaps she could bring along one or two of *Aeon Flux*'s costumes?

OLYMPIC TORCH: One of the great things about the new series is, you can sit down and watch it with normal people without feeling a sense of shame. Non-fans don't mind it when the Doctor hugs people and gives one of his exaggerated speeches about how great humanity is. And bizarrely, they actually seem to like the mushy romantic bits between him and Rose.

Just once in a while, though, there's a scene so cringe-worthy that you might as well be watching 'The Horns of Nimon'* One such scene could be witnessed in 'Fear Her'... Was there a solitary viewer over the age of seven who wasn't mortified by the supreme cheesiness of the Doctor lighting the loved-up Olympic flame with a torch of hope and peace, etc., to the accompaniment of that mawkish voiceover? Though, having said that, wouldn't it be lovely if the Olympic committee actually *did* hire David Tennant to light the flame in 2012? Maybe we should start a petition.

'ONE FOR A BOY, ONE FOR A GIRL': It's always been a mystery to us why the Doctor is a gay icon, so we're grateful to *Evening Standard* columnist John Little, interviewed on Radio 4's *Today* programme, for pointing out that it's because he has two hearts. Well, of course! How queer is that?!

Little also cited the Third Doctor's costume (fair enough – but it *was* the seventies) and the Fourth Doctor's uncanny ability not to fall upon a near-naked Leela at every opportunity. But then, the Fifth Doctor somehow managed to keep his hands off a pyjama-clad Adric and Turlough in trunks, so it looks like neither of those hearts is exactly working overtime. Hmm... to quote Jackie Tyler, 'Anything else he's got two of?'

---

* A wonderful story in many ways, but you wouldn't invite the neighbours round to watch the video. Unless you wanted to instigate some kind of feud with them, that is.

OOD: As we inadvertently seem to have established a theme of Welsh *Doctor Who* monsters looking like other things, it might not be too pedantic to mention the slight resemblance of the Ood to one of the creatures in the HP Lovecraft-based horror movie *Dagon*. Not to mention Dr Zoidberg from *Futurama*. Though the *TV Times* preferred to refer to them as 'Spag Bol Monsters' – ood'a thought it?

ORBITAL: Without waiting to be commissioned by the BBC or anything, some of the greatest talents in music have had a bash at covering the *Doctor Who* theme – Geoff Love and Mankind being just two of the names on the list. But it was the Hartnoll brothers (no relation to Billy, obviously) who put together the definitive arrangement as not heard on TV. And we were so certain that Eric Winstone and his Orchestra's classic sixties rendition would remain unsurpassed, we'd have put money on it.

ORGI: The Fourth Doctor's stony-faced adversaries, according to a pair of misprints on p62 of the novelisation of *Doctor Who and the Stones of Blood* (first edition).

OUR FRIENDS IN THE NORTH: Who'd have thought, when this classic drama originally aired in the early nineties, that just over a decade later two relatively unknown actors in its cast would be chosen to play Britain's greatest screen icons Doctor Who and James Bond? No sane casting director, that's for sure.

OVERSEAS VERSIONS: What with exotic and far-flung lands such as America (well, Canada, but it's the same thing really) and Wales having had a go at making the programme, we wondered if a few other countries might ever have wanted, say, a *Docteur Qui* of their own. After all, it's not like they're averse to remaking our sitcoms: there was a successful run of the Dutch *Steptoe and Son*, Australia had its own *Are You Being Served?* and the Germans did a version of *The Office* (without asking permission, apparently, but even so).

If nothing else it would be fun tracking down copies, and you never know, some might even be worth watching once you'd found 'em. For example, we've conducted extensive research into European culture (we watched some episodes of *Eurotrash*) and reckon the French one would be all arty, with the companion getting naked all the time, and the German one not so arty, but with the companion getting naked all the time (the Doctor too, probably).

TEN

Countries That Could Make Their Own Version of *Doctor Who* (We've Helpfully Suggested Actors to Play The Doctor Too)

1. France. Antoine de Caunes.

2. China/Hong Kong. Jet Li, or Sammo Hung if they adapt Sixth Doctor stories.

3. New Zealand. Not bothered really, as long as Lucy Lawless plays his companion.

4. Australia. George Lazenby. Then he really could be the *Doctor Who* equivalent of George Lazenby (see LAZENBY, GEORGE).

5. Swaziland. Richard E. Grant. Erm, well, perhaps not.

6. Holland. Rutger Hauer.

7. Iraq. Mohammed Saeed al-Sahhaf.

8. Germany. David Hasslehoff.

9. Italy. Roberto Begnini, or Steve Martin if he flops.

10. Scotland. Hmm... no, can't think of anyone who'd be right for it, really.

PAAARP: Noise made by the Slitheen Gas Exchange, the fantastic fart-maker provided with *Doctor Who Adventures #2*. It's really not fair – just as we were getting used to being able to pick up our *DWM*s with heads held high, it's back to brown paper bags at the checkout and the embarrassed pretence that we're buying for a young relative, honest.

Though we only get it for the free stuff*, *Doctor Who Fortnightly* could be a welcome addition to the sadly depleted line-up of British comics (especially since the *Dandy* started using artists presumably rejected by *2000 AD* for being too outlandish) – if only the art didn't look like it was done for an under-fives nursery comic. Being a BBC publication, it'd be no problem to obtain rights to monsters from the TV series – so, sadly, they're unlikely to create their own memorable recurring aliens like the Trods, the Kleptons or Beep the Meep. But they could include, say, a Space Pig backup strip and possibly pull-out centrefolds of Billie, though maybe we should be suggesting that to other mags instead? One advantage *DWA* does have over its older relative is that its behind-the-scenes features manage to cover in about twenty words what it takes *DWM* twenty pages to say.

---

* Nice try guys, but the stationery set with the first issue counts as one free gift, not six as claimed. Never mind, it was miles more generous than the measly transfers Marvel taped to the front of *Doctor Who Weekly*. See also **RADIO**.

PANINI: What *DWM* publishers Marvel UK call themselves these days. But 'Marvel' was a proper exciting name, promising a magazine full of... well, marvels. Panini is just a type of bread used in posh sandwiches, surely?

PAPARAZZI: Love 'em, hate 'em, let us just be grateful they were present on the beach the moment one of Billie Piper's fun bags tired of its restrictive, bikini-clad existence and made a successful bid for freedom in the sun (and indeed in *The Sun*).

PARSONS, NICHOLAS: Although mainly known for his quiz-hosting skills, he put in rather a good performance as Reverend Wainwright in 'The Curse of Fenric'. His acting seems even better in retrospect because his commentary for the DVD makes it plain he thought the story made no sense whatsoever. What's more, he's convinced that fans used their imaginations to fill in the plot holes and gaps in logic themselves. Good job he wasn't asked to play the vicar of that church in 'Father's Day': his brain would probably have exploded.

PARSONS, PAUL: Author of The *Science of Doctor Who* (was there some?). As editor of the science and technology magazine *BBC Focus*, he used the publication to promote his book (well, you would, wouldn't you? Though it's possible eight pages plus the cover was a bit OTT), but this led to claims that he might have breached BBC guidelines by doing so. Ironically, the fuss caused gave the book a whole load more publicity – but as it wasn't the BBC promoting the thing, it doesn't count.

PAUL McGANN ESTROGEN BRIGADE, THE: To judge from their website, a far more sane group of fangirls than the tongue-in-cheek name suggests. Which is a shame, as we'd hoped to get a few pages out of that one.

'PEACE AND LOVE': Memorable mantra of the Daleks, after they'd taken a break to gorge themselves on KitKats – though how they could fit two fingers of chocolate wafery goodness through those slats is beyond us. Obviously, this highly-budgeted TV and cinema advert in no way ruined the Dalek brand; we aren't talking about *Blue Peter* cakes, after all. To be fair, though, there's been a long and distinguished history of advertisers co-opting both the Daleks and their mortal enemy to flog unrelated wares. So long, in fact, that we're going to try for a super double-sized list as we run through the, er, prime examples.

20 Adverts That Did OK Out of *Doctor Who*

1. Weetabix got hold of a Dalek to advertise their fab *Who* give-aways of the seventies in a TV commercial. We could all have seen it again, but it was cut from the *More Than Thirty Years in the TARDIS* video as it would have constituted a free plug for the wheat-based product – and the BBC, obviously, only allow paid plugs. Not that fans would have been brainwashed into buying loads of Weetabix anyway. If they want us to do that, they'll have to put more monster cards and secret code messages in the boxes.

2. Panasonic persuaded Sylvester McCoy, Sophie Aldred and David Banks to advertise their batteries with a dramatic Cyberman adventure. We described it last time out, so suffice it to say it's the only *Doctor Who* radio story worthy of being deemed a classic – because it's much shorter than the others.

3. Twenty years before Renault named a vehicle after the Eighth Doctor (and called another the Espace – sad or what?), they turned to the Daleks – in an entirely non-ruinous way, we assume – to sell their wares. 'The Dalek Invasion of Renault' featured Terry Nation's creations in comic strip form, in search of the company's sophisticated technology. We'll never know if they found it, as the climactic conclusion was left open-ended (anyone who picked up a form was supposed to draw in the final panel themselves).

4. More cereal-based hard selling, as Kellogg's flew to New Zealand to record an advert for Cornflakes. The idea was to show that lots of interest groups had a mutual love for the prod-uct, and they got Andrew Beech of the *Doctor Who Appreciation Society* to prove it. Shame on him, though, for eating any cereal that didn't have one quarter of a *Doctor Who* game board on its packaging.

5. As BBV well know, a good way to procure the Doctor's servic-es without incurring bothersome copyright fees is to hire one of

the relevant actors to appear 'out of character'. That's why Tom Baker joined a list of *Tomorrow's World* presenters and other mock scientific luminaries to help British Telecom ring up a bit of profit in the early eighties. The Doctor's phone box, of course, never works, but we still like him. Perhaps the telecommunications giant was hoping to earn itself a similar reputation.

6. But Volkswagen went two better, when they required a *Doctor Who* analogy to emphasise the spaciousness of some car or other but resisted the urge to pay up for it. They had Jon Pertwee, Tom Baker and Peter Davison line up for the cameras – all out of costume, of course.

7. Tom must have done the business for BT, as they later borrowed a Dalek for a poster campaign to remind us how they'd selfishly added a '1' to every phone number in the UK. Their slogan was 'One to Remember' – and, appropriately enough, the gravel-voiced monster in question came from 'Remembrance of the Daleks'. Wonder if they knew?

8. Back when Tom Baker was the Doctor, the BBC used a host of monsters in a full-page newspaper promotion for their best-selling TV licences. The message, presumably, was that if you didn't pay your fee they'd send the boys round to duff you up.

9. Sugar Smacks did some terribly interesting thing or other to promote their *Doctor Who* badge giveaways of the mid-seventies. However, they seem to have lost the tape, so there's not much we can tell you about it.

10. How could we have reached the halfway point without mentioning Prime Computers? One of the best-known *Who*-related campaigns of all, this series of TV commercials from the land Down Under saw Tom Baker and Lalla Ward recreating their roles for the occasion. But then you knew that already, didn't you? Wonder what K9 would've thought if he'd caught his master and mistress shopping for replacements.

11. Almost as fondly remembered are those Antipodean anti-litter adverts, which entreated us to 'Keep Australia Beautiful' via pleas from a number of unseen characters including the Fourth Doctor's Australian cobber Darren and his sister Reylene.

12. Far less famous, though, is the Aussie advert for Ice Treat lollies. This animated epic, starring the Fourth Doctor (again) and K9, wins our vote for the best ever cartoon episode of *Doctor Who*. Sure, it's impossible to make sense of, but it's pretty clear to us that the Doctor defeats his foe – the dastardly ice man Necros – with the aid of an Ice Treat. Or something. By this point, it's beginning to look like Australians won't buy anything unless the Fourth Doctor tells them to.

13. Back to the UK, then, but sticking with lollies... Brilliant though the Sky Ray Space Raiders *Doctor Who* cards and book were, Walls lost all respect by getting some bloke who looked not a bit like Patrick Troughton to appear in the TV ad for them. Though he tried his best to hide his face with his hands, it just wasn't good enough. Mind you, the bloke they drew on the cards didn't look much like Pat either.

14. Yet one more company thought to associate the show with cars as, in 1989, the *Radio Times* carried a spread for the Mazda 121 Supermini, which asked the question 'How do you get a saloon-sized interior into a Mini-sized exterior?' The answer was provided by a picture of a TARDIS on wheels. But if what they say about cars is true, who wants an oblong, blue, wooden one?

15. Ah, how our stomachs are moved to tears as we recall the Nescafé advert that, true to the genre, recounted a coffee-centric episode in the domestic life of Peter Davison. It may not have been the Gold Blend couple, but the coffee was 'just what the Doctor ordered'.

16. Or, if coffee isn't to your taste, how about lager? Having already used SF icon Mr Spock on a poster, Heineken thought up the great wheeze of having a portaloo-shaped TARDIS dematerialise in one of their TV ads. Hilarious! If only they'd gone the whole hog and used that great 'TURDIS' joke...

17. Yet more telephones – and, not content with, er, paying homage to *The X-Files* and *Twin Peaks*, Vodafone hired Jon Pertwee to play a stranger who disappeared behind a 'Doctor on Call' sign in one of four 'spooky' adverts starring Kyle McLachlan and Toni Barry. We were tempted to include an entry for one of their earlier efforts too, as it featured the Loch Ness Monster; however, it looked nothing like the Borad, so we won't.

18. As recently as 2005, the Dalek brand was not ruined again by an Aussie ad for the ANZ bank, in which they teamed up with robots from *Lost in Space* and *Forbidden Planet* to answer phones in a call centre – the punch line being that if you call ANZ you'll get to speak to a real person as opposed to, er, well, being exterminated presumably.

19. Does anyone remember Peter Cushing extolling the benefits of milk on the set of *Doctor Who and the Daleks?* No, we don't either, but we do remember gratuitous plugs for Sugar Puffs in the sequel. Not that there was any actual product placement – unless those Robomen were scoffing Sugar Puffs in tablet form – just the odd poster suggesting that the staple diet of London's inhabitants in 2150 consisted of this sugary repast. We suspect some level of collaboration between the manufacturers and the would-be conquerors of Earth, culminating in a cereal-box opportunity to win a Dalek.

20. And of course we have the 1997 New Zealand commercials for life insurance, which featured Tom Baker in his honest-to-goodness Doctor persona reminding us (somewhat ominously) that time is running out. Tom himself suggested that a suitable slogan for the campaign could have been 'I've seen the future and you aren't there.' Perhaps he should have done some ads for the Samaritans while he was at it.

'PENIS-SHAPED HEADS': Possessed by the Sontarans, according to the *Daily Star*'s hilariously uninformed A to Z of *Doctor Who* monsters in March 2005. So, presumably, their journalists have potato-shaped penises.

PILOT FISH: Not the actual name of those Sycorax hangers-on of course. In 'The Christmas Invasion', their downfall was hastened by their proclivity for elaborate and insidious schemes, i.e., dressing up as Father Christmas and sneaking past the room in which the Doctor was unconscious to deliver a rotating tree. If they'd just nabbed him when they had the chance, they'd have been laughing.

PITT, INGRID: Two-time *Doctor Who* guest star, now often seen hawking nude photos of herself at collectors' fairs. Picture the scene: There you are, innocently strolling around in search of that one elusive Nestlés chocolate wrapper when suddenly your eyes are drawn to topless lesbian vampire photos. You look up, eventually, and are astonished to see the lesbian vampire herself sitting behind the stall. What to do? You'd quite like her autograph but is it all some kind of test? If you pick one of the nudie shots, is she going to lambaste you with accusations of being a filthy pervert? Remember, you've seen how Ms. Pitt deals with her victims in those films... So instead you go for a compromise. You buy the Strictly Ink autographed trading card featuring Ingrid in 'The Time Monster', and you pick up a copy of *The Vampire Lovers* on DVD – making sure it's the Region 1 edition, though, as you get to see a bit more of her in that.

TEN
Other *Doctor Who* Guest Stars Who've Got 'Em Out on Screen

1. The Inquisitor herself, Lynda Bellingham, got a bit rude in that classic of British cinema comedy *Confessions of a Driving Instructor*...

2. ...as did Sally Faulkner from 'The Invasion'. The film also featured Damaris Hayman of Miss Hawthorne fame, but thankfully she kept hers covered.

3. Sylvestra Le Touzel, the little girl in 'The Mind Robber', showed the lot in the third series of *Between the Lines*, but she was grown up by then, so it was OK to look.

4. Susan Penhaligon from 'The Time Monster'. In a couple of movies, actually. However, we recommend *Under Milk Wood*, if only for the Welsh connection.

5. Zoe Wanamaker proved herself less flat than Cassandra in the original *Prime Suspect*. Uniquely, however, star Helen Mirren (who, to maintain a bit of *Doctor Who* relevance, was once photographed alongside Tennant, Billie and a Dalek at the *Radio Times* cover party) kept hers in.

6. We have much to be grateful to Hammer Films for, and not least Virginia 'Dyoni from "The Daleks"' Wetherell's full frontal in

Demons of the Mind. And she gets even *more* naked in *A Clockwork Orange*.

7. Pauline Collins, a guest star in *Who* old and new, famously revealed her mighty pair in the film version of *Shirley Valentine*.

8. Barbara Windsor. The infamous bikini top-flinging scene from *Carry On Camping* is frequently revisited in retrospectives, and rightly so. However, more full-on views of Babs' baps from *Carry on Abroad* and *Carry on Dick* are shamefully ignored – they're what the DVD pause button was invented for.

9. Before she helped to make history in 'The King's Demons', Isla Blair made the BBC's *The History Man* a historical event.

10. And finally, *Art School Confidential* hasn't been released at the time of writing, but word has it that Sophia Myles plays an artists' nude model – which means it has the potential to be the greatest movie in the history of cinema.

PLAYING OUT: What Christopher Eccleston claims to have been doing instead of watching *Doctor Who* during his formative years. Smart kid.

'POINTLESSLY NORTHERN': The *People*'s verdict on the new series. You know, the one set mostly on a council estate in London.

POLICE BOX: Blimey, you have to watch those BBC lawyers. They only went and trademarked the design of the police box in 1996, with the police themselves not noticing for two years. It took another four for the case to get to court, with covers of *Doctor Who* videos and audios presented as evidence. For their part, the police could only offer up 'a photograph of a member of the public receiving "service" at the police box', which must have been interesting – though the fact that the box is *named after them* ought to have been a bit of a clue.

Evidently not, however, as the Beeb won the case and were awarded costs. The gist of the judgement seems to be that, as they never asked for permission to use the box, they weren't in breach of any agreement and therefore it must now be theirs to own. Er... no, can't quite see it. What next – copyrighting the image of Queen Victoria because it's there on the pub in *EastEnders* four times a week?

POLICE BOX DOORS: Seen inside the TARDIS in 'Rose', for the first time since the Peter Cushing movies. Though under the circumstances, revolving doors might have been more appropriate.

POLITICAL ALLEGORY?: Hey, did anyone else suddenly think, while watching 'Genesis of the Daleks' on DVD, that the Kaleds were a little bit like the Nazis from that World War thing? Nah, on second thoughts we probably just imagined in it when General Von Klinkerhoffen and Lt. Gruber out of *'Allo 'Allo!* turned up.

POWELL ESTATE, THE: The new series frequently 'touches base' here so that science-fiction-illiterate viewers can relate to its Earthbound normality (as opposed to Earthbound abnormality, we presume). But how can one be expected to relate to this perfectly horrid place? It's full of common oiks who dine on beans on toast and chips. See also **BEANS ON TOAST** and **CHIPS**.

PRISONER, THE: Seems every British fantasy show ever made has been mooted for a remake since *Doctor Who* reminded TV execs that the genre can be popular and cool and not at all embarrassing. But this one is of particular interest, because it was claimed for a brief time that Christopher Eccleston himself might star as Number Six in an updated version of the ITC classic. The rumour was denied – which is a pity really, as we could have pretended it was a reality show of sorts, with the actor playing himself in a Village populated by incensed *Doctor Who* fans (or 'Number Twos') demanding to know why he resigned. We could even have imagined that his '6' badge was a '9' badge accidentally inverted, and demanded a guest appearance by Number Eight.

TEN British TV Shows Probably Commissioned Only Because *Doctor Who* Was Popular

1. *Life on Mars.* Created by 'Fear Her's' Matthew Graham, and starring a time-travelling, leather jacket-wearing northerner and a whole Tyler family (who really were named after Rose). DCI Sam even claims to get his prescription drugs from Doctor Who

– though, given the time-travelling aspect, we're not sure if he means the Third or the Ninth.

2. *A for Andromeda.* B for Boring, C for Cheap, D for Dull, etc.

3. *Eleventh Hour.* ITV spent months making this look like a science-fiction series, only for Patrick Stewart to insist that it wasn't.

4. *The Quatermass Experiment.* We hear this was what David Tennant was doing when he learned he was to become the Tenth Doctor. And Mark Gatiss was naturally on hand to congratulate him.

5. *Hyperdrive.* So lamentably unfunny, it must surely have been the only SF comedy on the table when the BBC wanted one in a hurry. The producers even failed to deliver any eye candy: the male lead was the fat bloke off *Spaced* and the woman looked like Hagrid's sister.

6. *Robin Hood.* Heralded by the BBC as a Saturday evening family show in the *Doctor Who* mould, but sadly lacking in aliens and time travellers – though they'd probably all have picked Sherwood Forest to invade, anyway. Astonishingly enough, that sort of thing did go on in the American *New Adventures of Robin Hood* series of a few years ago – though not in any of the episodes in which Mary Tamm guest-starred, else we'd have watched it. The BBC show hasn't pleased many critics so far, but it did beat Ant and Dec in the ratings. Got the message yet, ITV execs? Proper. Imaginative. Drama.

7. *Johnny and the Bomb. Doctor Who*'s Keith Barron and Zoe Wanamaker appeared in this BBC adaptation of Terry Pratchett's novel. ITV had already made *Johnny and the Dead* from the same series of books a decade earlier (with *Doctor Who*'s George Baker and Brian Blessed). Different people played the kids in each series, though. Dunno why that should be – it's hardly consistent, is it?

8. *Primaeval.* Haven't seen this ITV series yet, but apparently it's nothing like *Doctor Who* and it's pure coincidence that it features a time-travelling doctor with a blonde former pop singer at his side. Anyway, if this is just an excuse to use the *Walking with Dinosaurs* technology, it's a pity. A proper follow-up to 'Invasion

of the Dinosaurs' could have benefited from the same.

9. *Torchwood*. Possibly not the soundest ever basis for a series – the fact that an anagram of *Doctor Who* makes an interesting word – but we quite like Captain Jack when he keeps his clothes on, so we'll see how it goes. At least we've been spared *Rose Tyler: Earth Defence*, which even Russell T admitted was 'a spin-off too far'. Pity the Beeb's commissioning editors couldn't have displayed the same admirable restraint. See also **TOTALLY DOCTOR WHO**.

10. *Ruby in the Smoke*. Another one we haven't seen, but the book is great and Billie's in the TV version so well worth a look.

PSYCHIC: What is the world coming to when a well-meaning fan can't make a sensible suggestion – such as hiring a psychic charlatan, possibly even Derek Acorah, to track down missing episodes of *Doctor Who* – on an Internet forum without being labelled 'barmy' in *The Sun*? To be fair, though, we suspect most of the Outpost Gallifrey posters also quoted in the article were being sarcastic. Must have been a slow news week again.

PUBLICITY POSTCARDS: Despite the sixteen-year gap between the old and new series, it's pretty much business as usual again for fans. Typically, in the old days, we'd read the Target novels and *Doctor Who Magazine* and buy our episodes on sell-thru VHS tapes, and we'd write off letters of praise to the BBC production office and in return receive lovely postcards autographed by members of the cast. Nowadays, the BBC novels are hardbacks, *DWM* is glossier, and the episodes come on shiny discs. But if you write to the BBC production office in Wales, the tight-fisted gits will send you bugger all! Sheesh, you'd think it was a BBC Scotland production! The annoying thing is that there are many lovely publicity postcards available, but only to the chosen few who get invited to press screenings and suchlike...

TEN

Ten *Doctor Who* Publicity Postcards You Most Likely Haven't Got*

1. The Ninth Doctor and Rose in front of the big fat TARDIS with London in the background. The first card produced by BBC Worldwide to publicise the Welsh series, it is now a very rare and desirable card for collectors. With its garish orange background, though, it looks bloody horrible.

2. The Ninth Doctor and Alison. Whoops, wrong Ninth Doctor. The Northern Doctor and Rose on a less rare, but nicer card.

3. Billie Piper as Rose. Lovely.

4. 'School Reunion'. Billie as Rose and Lis Sladen as Sarah Jane Smith – even lovelier.

5. A Dalek. Identical to the commercially available poster, only smaller, obviously.

6. Several Daleks. 'I wish Daleks were real,' it says on the back. Don't we all?

7. 'The Christmas Invasion'. 'Sycorax Strong. Sycorax Mighty. Sycorax Rock,' it says here. Hmm, quite.

8. 'New Earth'. It says 'Let us cure you,' and there's a picture of a cat nun on it. Wonder what they'll do now their hospital has been shut down? Maybe they'll carry on their medical work elsewhere; it depends whether they're creatures of habit. Geddit? Habit, they're nuns, see? Oh, please yourselves.

9. 'Tooth and Claw'. A sh*t-yer-pants scary one depicting the Werewolf silhouetted against the full moon, as the Doctor looks on.

---

* There's a *Doctor Who Confidential* card too. How the blummin' flip did that happen? Still, it's got Jackie on it so we'll let it go.

10. K9 (the rusty Mk3). K9 is no stranger to BBC postcards. Having initially had to share a black and white publicity card with the Fourth Doctor, he graduated to a solo colour card in the eighties. More recently, an illustrated BBCi postcard celebrated his return in the Paul McGann rehash of 'Shada'. Blimey, slipped into geek mode for a bit there.

PUSHING THE ENVELOPE: Although some stuff's better than others, it is just about possible to understand the appeal of almost every item of *Doctor Who* merchandise (though the *K-9 & Co.* theme music single presents a struggle). However, the interest shown in those so-called 'first day covers' is baffling. Sure, they're nicely designed and colourful and everything – but without a current *Doctor Who* stamp to stick on them, aren't they just really expensive envelopes?

QUEEN, THE: She's a bit of a fan, apparently. According to Prince Andrew, his mum used to watch *Doctor Who* and *Grandstand* with him every Saturday (no mention of *Basil Brush* though – perhaps Liz nipped off to make beans on toast while he was on). And more recently, Her Maj ordered the Series One box set to while away the hours on her Balmoral holiday. We should think she's about the only person with enough shelf space for the thing. Wonder if she's still so keen after that appalling slur on her family in 'Tooth and Claw'? (Princess Ann a werewolf? Eh? If they'd said 'were-horse', we could understand it...) We could make the obvious joke about how *Doctor Who* has always appealed to queens here, but we won't.

QUEEN'S ARCADE: See **GAY AGENDA**. Oh damn, we did it after all!

QUITTER, THE: Nickname bestowed upon Christopher Eccleston by some fans when they learned he was leaving the series. 'The audience's response for the new *Doctor Who* has been incredible and I am really proud to be part of it and I hope viewers continue to enjoy the series,' said someone at the BBC pretending to be the actor. 'The BBC... regrets that it falsely attributed a statement to Christopher and apologises to him,' Jane Tranter later added.

Meanwhile, the *Outpost Gallifrey* forums were temporarily shut down after a tidal wave of abusive postings. Look, really, to anyone out there who still thinks Ecclescake's decision shortened the programme's lifespan – meaning that, should *Doctor Who* still be a huge ratings winner when its thirteenth star quits, the Beeb will choose to axe it rather than contradict a line in 'The Deadly Assassin' – we have this message: *Yup, three more regenerations to go, and then THERE WILL BE NO MORE DOCTOR WHO EVER, EVER, EVER, so best just top yourself now and get it over with, yeah?*

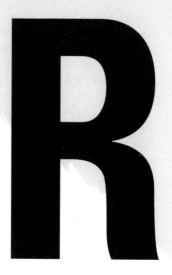

RADIO: Semi-rubbish free gift provided with *Doctor Who Adventures* #4. Or #3, if you got the Tesco exclusive edition from W H Smith. Or both, if you were careless. We say 'semi-rubbish' because, though it was fine as radios go, we don't see the *Who* connection. They could at least have slapped a logo on it – or shown the Doctor using it in the comic strip, perhaps in a rematch against the Turgids.

RADIO CONTROLLED NEW SERIES DALEK: Best! Toy! Ever!

RADIO TIMES: Here's an interesting statistic. Number of *Radio Times* covers devoted to *Doctor Who* during David Tennant's first series: Five. Number during the entire Tom Baker era, which we recall was quite popular too: None. Why the discrepancy? Could it be because, in the nineties, the magazine – which had been publishing BBC television and radio schedules since shortly after the Roman occupation of Britain – lost its listings monopoly and found itself competing with a myriad of similar yet cheaper publications?

Apart from one measly 'Five Doctors' cover, they hadn't wanted to know us in the eighties either – but now it was a different story, oh yes indeed. 'Dimensions in Time'; the telemovie (twice, in fact); we even got a Dalek (the same image used on the Dalek stamp) to celebrate BBC Two's *Doctor Who* night of a documentary and a few sketches.

By 2003, the *RT* were so keen to chase the fan pound that they didn't even need *Doctor Who* to be on the telly for it to grace their cover. Or covers, in fact – as, to celebrate the fortieth anniversary, they tried to flog us four copies of the same issue. Doctors Four, Five, Six and Seven featured on a set of specially-taken photos, which, when laid side by side, formed a larger image (of Doctors Four, Five, Six and Seven, obviously). Interestingly, Tom Baker and Peter Davison appeared in tasteful new outfits, which were merely suggestive of their TV costumes. Colin Baker and Sylvester McCoy, on the other hand, had to make do with the most horrible get-ups – their actual TV costumes. Fans questioned the absence of a Paul McGann cover – though at that point the BBC were trying quite hard to write his sole appearance out of history (a worthy ambition in many ways, but the evidence is out there on DVD). With the new series now so popular that even the formerly ITV-centric *TV Times* have stuck it up front (never thought we'd see the day), it must be like manna from heaven to the *RT* editors...

TEN *Radio Times* Covers for the New Series

1. OK, so it's cheating a bit – but two weeks before 'Rose', fan hearts skipped a beat at the image of a frilly-shirted, frock-coated David Tennant from *Casanova*, and next to him in block capitals, the words *DOCTOR WHO*. A poignant glimpse, we thought at the time, of what might have been. Now, it's proof that dreams can come true.

2. The fold-out TARDIS cover for the launch of the Christopher Eccleston Months, of course.

3. An unprecedented mid-series cover, which wittily combined the Daleks' return with the concurrent election campaign in the headline 'VOTE DALEK'. Sadly, they weren't standing in our constituency, else we would have done.

4. An actual Christmas cover – can you believe it? – with a snow-covered TARDIS, and that never happens. Well, hardly ever. No actual programme encroaches upon the generic festival frontage, it's simply not traditional.

5. 'Look Who's Back' – the gatefold Series Two cover, with Sarah and K9 and some monsters – and, ooh, get that CyberController, with its hand on its hips. It's like the spirit of Christopher Robbie's Cyber-Leader has returned.

6. And this year's mid-series excuse: the return of the Cybermen.

7. A dilemma here for the ardent collector: for the week of 'Army of Ghosts', the *RT* cover featured Billie Piper, but appearing as herself rather than in the guise of Rose Tyler. Not a *Doctor Who* cover, then, strictly speaking – should any future licensees produce new sets of postcards, trading cards or even another calendar of same, it's likely this one will be omitted – but it does have a relevance that makes it hard to ignore. The best way round this problem, we reckon, is to start a brand new collection of *Radio Times* covers featuring pretty girls with nice cleavages.

8. Another multiple cover for the Series Two finale, with the Daleks or...

9. ...the Cybermen. And in case you were wondering, those footballs toted by both were a nod to the fact that the World Cup Final was taking place on the same weekend as 'Doomsday'. Imagine our disappointment when the episode aired and the metal monsters failed to settle their differences with a kickabout. Or have those differences settled for them by the surprise appearance of another, far more fearsome, foe: the *Blue Peter* Football Monster!

10. Look, is it our fault if there's only been nine? Though by the time this book's out, there may have been a *Torchwood* cover and there could be another Christmas cover on the way... In fact, they'll probably just start doing *Doctor Who* covers all year round. The Easter edition could feature a Slitheen egg, *Life on Mars* could return with an Ice Warriors cover, etc.

RADIO TIMES COVERS, OLD: Missing from libraries up and down the country. Not the whole issues, mind, just the covers. And only the covers that featured *Doctor Who*, carefully torn away when no one was looking. Sometimes, it's painful to admit you have anything in common with some fans.

REDEMPTION: First Margaret Slitheen, then Cassandra... Russell T seems to have a penchant for creating unambiguously wicked villains, killing them off as they so richly deserve, then developing a fondness for them and bringing them back. Yet once returned, it seems that despite all the murder and villainy, they're quite nice really. Not sure we buy that. And why is it that the innocent Space Pig seems destined to remain dead?

REVERSIBLE CD SLEEVES: It never fails, does it! BBC Audiobooks were almost through the entire catalogue of 'missing' episodes when somebody thought a packaging redesign would be a good idea (it wasn't). But never mind, because at least they provided reversible covers for collectors to maintain uniformity. Not on 'The Invasion', though. Sheesh, it was taking the mickey (not that one) in the first place bringing it out on triple CD when only two episodes are absent from the archives, but this was too much. As soon as the DVD with the cartoons is out, those CDs are going straight back in that Cybertin, never to see the light of day again.

REVIVALS: Blimey – new *Doctor Who*, *New Captain Scarlet* and new *Quatermass* all on in the same week. It's almost like getting into a TARDIS and going back to a time when, erm, *Doctor Who* and *Captain Scarlet* were on telly and... oh, *Quatermass and the Pit* was on at the cinema. Or something.

RICKY: How we sneered at those obsessive fans who insisted there was some deeper significance to the Northern Doctor's nickname for Mickey, rather than it just being that he was a condescending nob. And then, thanks to 'Rise of the Cybermen', those fans were proved right. Don't you hate it when that happens?

ROOM 101: Entertainment show on which, not content with having cancelled *Doctor Who* some thirteen years earlier, an unrepentant Michael Grade made the series his first choice to be banished into the Orwellian room. He dismissed repeated boos and hisses from the audience by suggesting they were all fans anyway – apparently he'd seen 'the hush puppies and the National Health glasses'. Insulting, yes, but maybe he felt entitled after the '*Doctor Who Appreciation Society of America*', so he claimed (we've never heard of it), made him the recipient of a special Horse's Ass Award.

However, Grade did confess to a hatred for science-fiction in general – so apparently his philosophy as BBC One Controller was that the publicly-funded channel should only cater to his personal tastes. *Room 101* host Paul Merton pointed out that, at the time of its axing, *Doctor Who* was getting more viewers than *Wogan* or *Match of the Day* – but after clips of Bok, the Kandyman and Ingrid Pitt karate-kicking the Myrka were displayed, the show's fate was sealed. Not even the most ardent hush puppy wearers in the audience dared lift a hand to spare it.

ROSE: What a dog, and a complete bitch! The parallel universe version, we mean. For the other one, see **TYLER, ROSE.**

TEN Companions Who've Been Name-Checked in Episode Titles

1. Rose. In 'Rose'. An easy one to start you off, there.

2. Steven, in 'The Feast of Steven'. Ahh, you see what they did there? They misspelled 'The Feast of Stephen' to imbue it with a clever double meaning.

3. Ace, in various episodes including 'The Space Museum', 'The Space Pirates', 'Frontier in Space', etc. Not to mention 'The Face of Evil', 'The Faceless Ones'... What do you mean, it's cheating? The letters are all there; it counts.

4. Similarly, Mel Bush's name appears in the title 'Timelash'. Or 'The Ambush' (which is an episode of 'The Daleks', as if you needed telling).

5. Remember Emma – Julia Sawalha's companion to the Ninth, Tenth, Eleventh, Twelfth and Thirteenth Doctors in 'The Curse of Fatal Death'? Good. Because she gets a name check in 'The Twin Dilemma'. Oh yes, she does.

6. And so does Ian, in 'The Talons of Weng-Chiang'. Just near the end there.

7. And Peri, in 'The Sontaran Experiment'.

8. Now, you really have to bear with us here, but... Remember Bernard Cribbins' character in *Daleks Invasion Earth 2150AD*? Remember what he was called? That's right – Tom. As in 'Tomb of the Cybermen'. Or, even better, 'The End of Tomorrow' – which is an episode of 'The Dalek Invasion of Earth', on which *Daleks Invasion Earth 2150AD* was based. Spooky, eh?

9. Oh lordy, er... all right then, Chang Lee, from the telemovie – see how his arrival was foreseen over three decades in advance when 'The Reign of Terror' part three was christened 'A Change of Identity'. 'Change' you see, because it has the letters 'Chang' in it. Um...

10. And, although 'Johnny Ringo' ('The Gunfighters' part three) seems to refer to another character altogether, its first four letters could easily be a big-up to the Doctor's grandchild John in the alternative universe of *TV Comic*. Though, of course, if you accept that John and Gillian had the surname Who, then that also allows 'Doctor Who and the Silurians', 'The Death of Doctor Who'... Oh, all right then, moving along...

ROSE'S PHONE(S): See **DAVIES EX MACHINA**.

ROSIE: The name of Billie's character according to everyone's local newspaper, *The Metro*. We kind of like it, actually. When 'Rosie' left the show, the *Metro*'s psychics helpfully gazed into their balls to predict whether Billie had made a good judgement call, and apparently she had; possibly she'll go on become one of Britain's top actresses. Oh dear, and we were hoping she'd have to resort to porn. On the down side, with her 'Mars in Scorpio' (we bet Vila ate it), Billie's love life may not be such a smooth ride. Hmm, even the least mystic of us could have made that forecast simply by reading *The Star*, never mind the stars.

RUBBISH: Our humble opinion of every single fan-made so-called comedy extra that has dragged down the level of what might otherwise have been a near-perfect DVD. Look, we know there must be a temptation to include them – especially when there's some brilliant acting such as Jeremy Bentham's spot-on portrayal of Sidney Newman – but in future, guys, stick to extras that are more entertaining and essential. Arabic soundtracks, for example. The place for the other kind of thing is a convention late at night, when the punters are too drunk to care.

RUBY WAX SHOW, THE: TV show hosted by Ruby Wax – obviously – but of note to fans because, a few years back, it boasted an unscheduled appearance by none other than curvy Katy Manning. 'Kate Manning... the first *Doctor Who* girl,' as she was introduced, popped up during a filmed interview with Liza Minelli – her best friend, apparently – and both were daft as brushes. 'I don't understand this interview that you're about to see,' confessed Wax, before showing us footage of Katy crawling on the floor, singing Christmas carols, impersonating her primary school teacher and giggling. A lot. After Katy and Liza re-enacted their first meeting, however, the host seemed to get the idea: 'You were, like, young nymphomaniacs!'

SALAMANDER: Often mistaken for the Second Doctor by cover artists.

SARAH JANE AND ROSE – HOW THAT CONVERSATION MIGHT HAVE GONE: 'I've seen things you wouldn't believe.' 'Try me.' 'Spiders on strings!' 'A transsexual trampoline!' 'Vacuum cleaner heads – lots of them!' 'Farting babies – in Downing Street!' 'Grey Daleks!' 'Got the bronze!' 'Green bubble-wrap!' 'Rejects from *The Matrix*!' 'Bad CSO!' 'Bad CGI!' 'A five-foot tall willy!' 'What, seriously?'

SATAN: As fundamentalist Satan worshippers, we were greatly offended by the events depicted in 'The Impossible Planet' and 'The Satan Pit'. In real life, the Dark Lord would easily kick Doctor Who's arse in a fight. By way of protest, we intend to march on Cardiff, burn some issues of *Doctor Who Adventures*, wave some insulting banners about the place, and possibly sacrifice a virgin too, provided we can find one there.

SATELLITE CITY: Nineties sitcom from BBC Wales in which Nick Courtney, having been unable to appear in *Recall: UNIT*, finally got to drag up. But then, who watches anything made by BBC Wales?

SATO, TOSHIKO: A brief glimpse of Naoko Mori's legs in 'Aliens of London' seemed to drive quite a number of forum posters wild with desire. Get a grip, lads! But before you do, perhaps an issue or two of *Asian Babes* are in order – if you can reach the top shelf, that is. The boys

will be ecstatic that Doctor Sato is back as a *Torchwood* regular – almost as happy as the paper tissue manufacturers, no doubt.

SCI-FI CHANNEL: America eventually bought new *Doctor Who* – hooray! They put it on the Sci-Fi Channel – doh! It's hardly NBC is it? In fact the nearest British equivalent would be, erm... oh yeah, the Sci-Fi Channel. Nearly forgot about that one.

SECRET OF GERMANY VS. ENGLAND, THE: A brave attempt, back in 2001, to unite the worlds of *Doctor Who* and football. Big Finish Doctor Jon Culshaw starred as both the Time Lord (fourth incarnation) and his soccer-pundit foe, Motty. Also appearing were Jeremy Clarkson, Russell Crowe's *Gladiator* and a few other people whose voices Culshaw can do. The Doctor revealed that he'd once been offered the job of England manager – cor, now it doesn't even have to be an Earthman – but was surprisingly coy about revealing the outcome of the next England/Germany match. Not that you needed a TARDIS to predict that one.

SEX/NUDITY: There's 'some', albeit of the 'mild' variety, of this stuff in 'The Tomb of the Cybermen', according to the back of the DVD. We've scrutinised the episodes repeatedly, but can't find it. Maybe the caution was included out of deference to Victoria, who showed her shapely ankles for the first time in this story. And yet why is there no similar warning on 'The Aztecs', despite the starring role played by Walter Randall's belly button in the *Remembering the Aztecs* documentary?

SEX TARDIS: We haven't a clue what this is supposed to be, but apparently the lovely Billie stepped out of one to do some pictures for *Arena* magazine. Some were really nice piccies too, if a little tame, but others were just headshots! What's the point of those, then? Bring back *Girl Illustrated*, we say.

SEXIEST MAN IN THE UNIVERSE: Accolade awarded to David Tennant by *The Pink Paper** in 2006; he beat off Brad Pitt in second place, with David Beckham coming up behind in third. See also *FHM*.

SHAKESPEARE, WILLIAM: Rumour has it he'll be back in the next series. Well, as long as he's still played by Hugh Walters from 'The Chase'... Also, we can't really imagine the Tenth Doctor being familiar with Shakespeare's works – *Heat* magazine, yes; the Bard, no.

---

* Obviously not a publication we peruse ourselves – though we are surprised the *Financial Times* hasn't more important fiscal matters to cover.

SHEEN, MICHAEL: Among many other roles, he played Kenneth Williams brilliantly in *Fantabulosa!* He's been named by Russell T as a favourite choice for a future Doctor – but then, in the same interview, Russell claimed he'd have no hesitation in casting a woman in the role. Yeah, right, course you would! Go on then, dare you – you could have the Doctor regenerate on an oestrogen-rich planet or something. We don't know why the press still fall for this old chestnut – this time, they even bought into the idea that Billie Piper might play the Time Lord! – but they do. Though at least the *Guardian*'s Lucy Mangan put the case against, citing among her reasons the fact that a publicity campaign would be necessary 'explaining to Whovians what a woman is'. Yeah, nice one Lucy.

SHIPPERS: Mostly female subculture of fandom – and therefore one that hasn't really existed for *Doctor Who* before now, being more of a *Star Trek* or an *X-Files* thing. Their only interest in the show seems to be the hope of the lead characters getting it on – 'relation-shippers', do you see? Apparently, it makes them go 'squee'. Or something.

And if it doesn't happen on screen, well then, they're more than happy to compose their own romantic fiction with pairings like the Eighth Doctor and Grace, the Northern and Tenth Doctors and Rose – even, in some cases, male and female incarnations of the Doctor. Then there are the 'Mary Sues', who include thinly-veiled (in more ways than one) versions of themselves in their stories, enjoying passionate moments with the dreamy Doc. We're even getting 'slash fiction' now, in which two male characters get it on. In *Star Trek*, it was usually Kirk and Spock, but an entirely random *Doctor Who* example might feature Captain Yates and Adric. There doesn't seem to be a specific term for girl on girl action, though – and sadly, apart from Xena/Gabrielle escapades, this doesn't seem to feature too much in fan-written tales.

TEN 'Ships' We'd Like to See in the TV Series

1. Bloody none, in fact.

'SILLY DICK': We weren't imagining this, were we? Basil Brush really was subjected to this shocking insult by his human sidekick, Roy North, in the Yeti sketch featured on 'The Mind Robber' DVD?! A bit harsh, we thought...

SIMMONDS, JAKE: Ricky's gay lover, in early versions of 'Rise of the Cybermen' and 'The Age of Steel' (see **GAY AGENDA**) – and, though this relationship was supposedly excised, it still comes across quite strongly when Jake learns of Ricky's death. Good job Mickey made it clear he wasn't taking over where his counterpart left off, or that visit to Gay Paree could have been a real eye-opener. You might say we're reading too much into the subtext, but perhaps the lesson is this: If you want to imply that a character's straight, you don't get a Children's BBC presenter to play him.

SIXTY-TWO SECONDS: Length of time it now takes – thanks to the BBC logo, the 2 Entertain logo, the copyright notice and the endlessly fascinating menu animation – from putting a *Doctor Who* DVD in your player to being able to play the damn thing. What's that you say, you can skip past all that stuff on the R1 discs? No way! And if you want to watch a new-series episode, that'll be seventy-six seconds out of your life, thank you very much. We could rewind our old VHS tapes faster!

SLITHEEN: Alien family who seem to share a common ancestry with CITV's Boohbahs.

SMITH, SARAH JANE: How fitting that this most popular of companions was selected to tie the new series to the old. It just wouldn't have been right if her TV swansong had been in 'Dimensions in Time', dressed like the rejected fourth member of Rod, Jane and Freddy. It's also fantastic that Lis Sladen somehow looks younger and even lovelier now than she did thirteen years ago. In fact, it's nothing short of a miracle. Incidentally, we hear that upon returning to the *Doctor Who* set, Lis promptly sprained her ankle. That's what we call a method actor!

'SOFAS ARE UP AGAINST WALLS – HOW DO YOU GET BEHIND THEM?': Lovely to see this ages-old myth finally exploded by David Tennant on *Blue Peter*. Can't see it making much difference, though. You may as well try to tell lazy presenters that Daleks can climb stairs these days.

'SOME OF THE BEST DOCTOR WHOS': Stars of *The Sun*'s April 2006 collection of free *Doctor Who* DVDs, according to Sylvester McCoy in the voiceover for the TV ad. Unfortunately, he wasn't one of them. Unlike our favourite non-existent actor Peter Davidson, who starred in their version of 'Earthshock' part one. There were no episodes for Doctors Six or Eight either – though this was arguably not a rare instance of the paper showing good taste, but more likely because they ran out of days of the week.

Actually, we're gutted they didn't take the opportunity to release 'Remembrance of the Daleks' part one with the proper effects. We're also unconvinced by the logic of distributing surviving episodes of 'The Daleks' Master Plan' and 'The Faceless Ones' to potential new fans. 'If you enjoyed this episode and want to see the rest of the story... well, tough.'

'SOMETIMES YOU LET ONE GO': Philosophy of Blon Fel Fotch Passameer-Day Slitheen, expressed in 'Boom Town'. Or another fart gag, we're not sure.

SONIC SCREWDRIVER: See **DAVIES EX MACHINA**.

TEN Useless Gadgets

1. The Silurians' Third Eyes. No smutty innuendo, please – we're thinking of those useful organs possessed by the original Silurians, which doubled as handy heat blasters. Not so their eighties counterparts, who turned the eye into a more functional light bulb to flash in time with their words and make them look cool.

2. The Brigadier's Computer. Sighted in Omega's lair, and wrong in so many respects. The first being that the machine was from the Doctor's lab; the second, that the Brig was hardly a computer sort of a bloke. But most of all, because this free-standing box with dual tape reels can surely only have hailed from Graeme Garden's corner of the Goodies' office.

3. The Time Lords' black and white televisions, from the same story. Perhaps they just thought Billy Hartnell would look somehow wrong in colour.

4. The Bandrils' Bendalypse Warhead. A Weapon of Mass Destruction, apparently, and nothing to do with having a flexible mouth at all. Though as the TARDIS survived a direct hit from one without a trace of an explanation, it can't have been much cop either way.

5. The Master's Tissue Compression Eliminator. If it only compresses tissue, why do peoples' clothes shrink with them, and how could the Doctor murder Kamelion with it? Presumably the sight of a naked, shrunken Master running around Sarn was considered too much by the production team – though given some of the other scenes in 'Planet of Fire', we can't see why.

6. The Master's other machine, from 'Frontier in Space' – you know, the one that made people see their greatest fears. So, Draconians saw humans and vice versa – but what about those members of either race who had a pre-existing phobia? Surely someone must have seen the cloaked Ogrons as, say, an army of spiders or a confined space? Just one report along the lines of 'We were pursued and boarded by an unbearable futility of mortal existence', and the scheme would have been exposed. Still, we shouldn't mock, as the device did have one extraordinary effect upon us while watching the video of this story. When the Master turned it towards the screen at the end of part five, we suffered the terrifying delusion that the bubbly electronic alternative Pertwee theme had made it onto an episode.

7. The TARDIS's scanner. Quite useful, actually, so long as you remember to use it instead of just blundering out to be cut down by a hail of bullets. But the real question is, why was it trained upon Nyssa's bedroom in 'Terminus'?

8. Sarah Jane's Menstrual Cycle. We don't know much about this, cos the only mention of it was censored from the Missing Adventure *Evolution* for reasons of good taste (surely the only time that ever happened in a Virgin book). We're informed, however, that it's a 'woman's thing', which probably means it's one of those girly affairs with a high saddle and pink handlebars. Quite right, then. Sarah would have looked ridiculous pedalling into battle against intergalactic despots on that.

9. The Doctor's TARDIS sniffer-outer. All right, so we only put this one in because it resembles a meat and two veg, especially when

Jo cradles it in her lap and it looks like she's trying it on for size. And this in a story that already featured a TOMTIT.

10. The Valeyard's Megabyte Modem. Funny how, in 1986, this sounded almost passably futuristic – well, Pip and Jane Baker must have thought so – whereas now it sounds like something you'd connect to the Internet with. Speaking of which, Michael Jayston once told us he refused to say the line 'You blundering imbecile, you've triggered a ray phase shift!' until the writers assured him it was scientifically accurate. Right...

SONIC SCREWDRIVER TOY: Yes, it's very nice indeed and looks just like the real one off the telly. But remember, like it says on the box, it's a toy, merely a bit of plastic that lights up at the end. Which means that ostensibly grown-up people ought not to take it out with them everywhere and aim it at things, especially in the pub where they can embarrass their friends. Yes, Jason, we do mean you (and that scarf's a bit much in the summer, too).

SPACE: What the S in TARDIS stands for. Just a reminder. In case anyone's forgotten lately.

SPACE PIG: The greatest ever character in televised *Doctor Who* – and in fact vying with *The Muppet Show*'s Pigs in Space and the hero of Walter R Brooks's book *Freddy and the Space Ship* for the title of Best Space-Faring Porcine in Fiction. We were gutted when he bought it, as he really deserved his own spin-off series. But look on the bright side: bacon butties all round!

TEN Tastiest Monsters

1. The Space Pig. There was, of course, an earlier Space Pig in *Doctor Who*: Mr Sin, the Peking Homunculus – he looked a sight less appetising, though.

2. The Dryrth, from the *DWM* comic strip – Space Cows!

3. The Ergon – Space Chicken!

4. The Kandyman.

5. The Macra.

6. The Gastropods, if you fancy a bit of French cuisine. They'd probably eat Urbankans' legs too, the filthy swine.

7. The prawn-like Nucleus of the Swarm, perhaps in a nice curry or a seafood pizza.

8. The Werewolf (Jessica Martin version, not the cartoon one). Yum.

9. The Krynoids, maybe, if vegetables are your thing.

10. The Sisters of Plenitude, a delicacy in Korea.

SPIDER DALEKS: Oft-rumoured makeover for the metal meanies from Skaro. First we were going to get them in the telemovie, then everyone seemed to think they'd be turning up in the Welsh series. They even got a fan-pleasing outing in the PDA *War of the Daleks*. The main drawback to the idea, as we see it, is this: Daleks are Dalek-shaped. That's why they're called Daleks. Make them spider-shaped, and they cease to be Daleks. So let's hear no more on the subject.

SPINAL CRAP: Not so long ago, it was possible to stand back and admire our shelves of *Doctor Who* DVDs and suffer only mild palpitations due to the occasional pictorial faux pas. You know the kind of thing: Patrick Troughton appearing in black and white on 'The Seeds of Doom' but in colour on the others, Doctors Four to Seven having different photos on their debut releases, etc.

Then suddenly, without warning, it appeared: the aesthetic nightmare that is the 2 Entertain logo. OK, deep breaths, stay calm, remember how they changed the design of the VHS cases partway through the run, you got through that trauma unscathed, give or take the odd mental scar...

SPOCK, MR: Unlike Arthur Dent, the *Enterprise*'s First Officer seems to be a fictional character in the *Doctor Who* universe. Which is just as well, else he could have sued the Tenth Doctor for nicking his mind-meld techniques. Presumably, the Doctor picked them up from Vulcan too – but the one in 'The Power of the Daleks'.

STEVENS, RACHEL: What is it with this former S Club 7 singer and

Doctor Who? First, she was up for the part of Rose ('But I think it was good that I didn't get it,' she said, echoing the sentiments of a grateful nation), then Rose's replacement, then a regular in *Torchwood*, each time accompanied by a blaze of self-publicity. 'I so hope I get it,' said the lovely Rachel on the *Torchwood* role, 'as I'm sick of being attacked for my music.' To cheer her up, then, we suggest that everyone watch the various *S Club* TV series and drop her a note about her acting ability.

STICKER ALBUM (AND STICKERS TO GO IN IT): Another long overdue bit of merchandise, produced by Merlin though we'd have put money on Panini doing it. Older fans should be warned not to attempt to fill the album following an evening in the pub; a look at their handiwork the following day will demonstrate just how tricky it is to get the corners right. This is not intended to be amusing, it's a serious warning based on personal experience. Also, in the grand old seventies tradition, you can send off for the last few stickers at a cost of 7p each, instead of buying hundreds more packs and never getting the damn things. Producers of trading cards, take note.

STRING 'EM UP: So, Russell T would have 'despised' a Doctor who'd taken someone to a death sentence. OK – what should he have done? Because waiting for your condemned foe to turn into an egg won't work every time (we hope). In fact, Margaret Slitheen presents a pretty compelling argument in favour of capital punishment: already guilty of attempted genocide twice over, she attempts murder even as she claims to be a reformed character. And let's face it, death is the usual penalty for anyone who dares cross our hero, whether it be by acid bath, compost grinder or, in the majority of cases, explosion. Liberal? Yeah, right!

And the Welsh series is no different. Look what the Doctor did to Cassandra, and the Sycorax leader, and the Krillitanes... Only once that we can recall did the hanging Time Lord 'let one go', and that was when he caught the Chameleons kidnapping holiday-making youths for their bodies, made them promise not to be naughty chameleonic life forms again and sent them packing. Surely, once out of his sight, they would have got straight back to business on another world? Oh no, you might say, because we never had any more trouble from them – but then, how would we know?

Oh, and then there's 'The Mark of the Rani', in which the Doctor intimated that he might punish the Master and the Rani's joint slaughter of innocents on Earth by marching them into the latter's TARDIS and telling them to just sod off the planet. But we like to think that, on this occasion, he'd fixed things to ensure their deaths at the claws of that tyrannosaurus. He was in his sixth incarnation, after all...

STUPIDITY OF THE DALEKS: OK, so the Doctor's building an all-powerful Delta Wave, whatever that is, with which he can wipe out your entire race but only at the expense of taking the innocents of Earth with you. Let's reflect on that for a moment: *The only thing keeping you alive is the fact that there are people on Earth.* So... what is the most brainless, idiotic thing you could do? Choose this moment, after centuries in hiding, to start vaporising continents and slaughtering human beings wholesale? Yup, we reckon so. No humans left = no reason for your mortal enemy not to flip that switch. Unless, by some fluke, he's even more stupid than you are.

SUBSCRIPTION: What the *Radio Times* helpfully advised its readers to take out, to ensure they didn't miss its free exclusive *Doctor Who* wall chart and stickers. Although grateful for the suggestion, we feel bound to point out that all we actually needed to do was buy four weekly issues. Not much of a challenge, then, for experienced merchandise collectors such as ourselves... er, we mean saddoes who want all that stuff. Nice try, though.

SWANSEA: Welsh city that infamously stood in for Cardiff in 'The Unquiet Dead', while Cardiff was busy standing in for the rest of the universe. Worked on us, though; we could have sworn those exterior scenes were Cardiff-shot – if only because they somehow managed to look like a studio set.

SYCORAX: The seventeenth moon of Uranus. Tsk! One-track mind, that Russell T Davies. See **CAPTAIN JACK'S ARSE**. And **GAY AGENDA**.

T: Did you know that Russell T's middle initial doesn't stand for anything? He uses it to differentiate himself from some radio presenter. Though, after enduring 'The Long Game', we thought of at least a couple of appropriate words.*

TALKING CYBERMAN: Excellent model from Product Enterprises, which comes programmed with four phrases: 'Mmmmmm Mmmmm', 'Mmmmmmmmmm', 'Mmmmmmmmmm mmm Mmmm Mmmm' and 'Mmmmmmm mm m mmmmmmmm'. We used to think this was an unfortunate mistake – but after 'Rise of the Cybermen', it seems uncannily prescient.

TARDIS: The Doctor's dimensionally transcendental ship. It was presumably immune to the pull of the rift in 'Doomsday', so Rose and Jackie could have taken shelter inside it and spared everyone a lot of heartache.

TAXICAB LOGO: Picture the scene: it's the morning of the meeting to decide on the new *Doctor Who* logo, but the designer has done no work. He's starting to panic when his black cab turns up. He spots the illuminated taxi sign, and suddenly there's a moment of inspiration. He whips out his crayons, and seconds later his job is done!

But no, we're being unfair – because if you think about it, the new series logo is actually very clever. The producers of Welsh *Doctor Who* are

---

* Terrific, tremendous, talented. What did you think we meant?

keen to suggest that the Doctor could arrive in our lives and whisk us away on adventures, if only we're good enough. So, that logo is surely designed to plant a subliminal suggestion that maybe we *could* just flag down the big fat TARDIS and get on board. There – bet those sane and rational fans who e-mailed abuse to the design studio are kicking themselves now.

TEN Doctors and the Official BBC Designations (Possibly) for Their Respective Logos

1. William Hartnell: The OHO logo. Not so much a logo, more a drab typeface. Even World Distributors couldn't be bothered using it, which possibly explains their '*Dr Who*' annuals.

2. Patrick Troughton. The Troughton logo. Jazzed up to become a drab typeface with serifs.

3. Jon Pertwee. Hooray, a proper one at last (though World still didn't think so). Followed by the diamond logo – which, oddly enough, didn't always include the diamond-shaped bit when featured on merchandise.

4. Tom Baker: The diamond logo and the neon logo.

5. Peter Davison: The neon logo.

6. Colin Baker: The neon logo, but with a bit of a bend in it.

7. Sylvester McCoy: The McCoy logo. Formerly known as the crap logo, until the new series came along. It was so rubbish that as soon as McCoy went, pretty much everyone reverted to using the iconic diamond logo (usually with the diamond intact).

8. Paul McGann: The Pertwee logo. This shiny variation has of course been ubiquitous on *Doctor Who*-related stuff for the past decade. That's just original series products though – or 'classic

Who' as some people now like to call it, even when referring to, for example, 'The Two Doctors' on DVD.

9. Christopher Eccleston: The taxicab logo. It looks a bit like the *Farscape* logo too, though less stylish.

10. David Tennant: The taxicab logo. You'd think that, if David was enough of a geek to insist on being credited as the Doctor rather than Doctor Who, he could at least have asked for a nice new logo of his own.

TEACH YOURSELF DALEK IN SIX EASY LESSONS: Erroneously titled bits of padding in the 'Genesis of the Daleks' DVD documentary. These consist of Roy Skelton reading out Dalek dialogue, in English, in the voice of Zippy from *Rainbow*.

TEARS: Gosh, the Doctor cried real tears after bidding farewell to Rose; he really must have reciprocated her love. Yeah, right. And just a few weeks earlier, he was ready to bin her off for that French chick who had a bit more going on upstairs (brains, we mean, not knockers).

TELOS NOVELLAS: Things have been quite busy in the literary arena since we playfully mocked Virgin's New and Missing Adventures a decade ago. Having their own publishing arm and noticing that Virgin had an ever-expanding library of *Doctor Who* books, the penny finally dropped at the BBC. And so, a mere three decades after Fredrick Muller published the first *Who* novel, BBC Books began a range of their very own – which were basically just like the Virgin ones but with even worse covers. How on earth, then, did they end up farming out the licence again, while their EDAs and PDAs were ongoing? Calling them 'novellas' and banging on about how they're an entirely different format, no really, fooled no one. And after a cracking start by Kim Newman, the Telos line just seemed to turn into the BBC/Virgin line, only with fewer pages for more money. It's debatable whether the covers were any less attractive, though.

TEN-INCH, DAVID: Billie Piper's very special nickname for her latest co-star – though, in a statement he must have found disheartening, she confessed, 'I have no basis or grounds for calling him that.' We suggest she take a look at the Series 2, Volume 1 DVD cover – though obviously, we're hoping that it's just his sonic screwdriver! We almost found out for sure when *The Sun* broke the 'news' that David had stripped off on stage just eleven years earlier – but they slapped a TARDIS over his tackle on the accompanying photo. We haven't seen it ourselves, so we don't know if it was an old-series TARDIS or a new one... Come to think of it, Noel Clarke also claimed to be 'proud of what I'm packing' in a *DWM* interview, while John Barrowman launched into a series of bagpipe-related double entendres for ITV's *Loose Women* ('the pipes are long enough for four and I can hold plenty in my bags'), as well as claiming to be 'bigger [than Tom Cruise] in a lot of areas'. Hmmm. Perhaps a valuable insight, there, into the process by which the show casts its leading men.

'THE FIRST TIME DOCTOR WHO'S HAD A BLACK ASSISTANT': BBC News's take on the casting of Freema Agyeman in the week before 'Doomsday'. Which suggests they can't have been watching too closely, and must have cheesed off Noel Clarke – not gone, but forgotten. And what about Alison Cheney, Roz Forrester and Sharon from Blackcastle? Or, er, Frobisher? The Beeb also described Freema as a 'newcomer' – like *Crossroads* doesn't count or something. Oh, well, maybe they've got a point there. See also **JONES, MARTHA.**

'THERE MAY BE PLENTY OF ROOM INSIDE, BUT HOW DO WE GET THIS STUFF THROUGH THE DOOR?': Caption from Jason Lythgoe-Hay's cartoon in *Doctor Who Magazine* #346, which showed the newly-cast Christopher Eccleston (presciently not dressed like the Doctor at all) and Billie Piper struggling to move their furniture into the TARDIS. Days later, the new-look TARDIS was unveiled, and the question answered.

THREE-D GLASSES: Used for spotting Dark Materials, erm, we mean Void Stuff. Pity, that – as, after seeing the glasses in 'Army of Ghosts', we were quite drawn to the notion that Rose had played a cracking spec-swapping wheeze on the Doctor, and he hadn't realised he was going round looking like a complete tit.

THROUGH TIME: It's rare nowadays that we learn much new from yet another *Doctor Who* factual book – so hats off to Andrew Cartmel for teaching us that, in fact, all the stories we thought were quite good are actually rubbish, and that all the ones he script-edited are the true classics, albeit sometimes spoilt by lesser talents. Must've been our memories cheating again.

TIM IS GAY: 'Cheeky subliminal message' sneaked into *DWM* #360's Production Notes via the first letter of every paragraph. Russell T obviously likes that sort of thing, as he later persuaded the *Radio Times* to do the same with the phrase 'A Cup of Tea' in their 'Christmas Invasion' preview. But who's Tim? Surely not Tim Brooke-Taylor of *The Goodies*, we're not having that! Maybe the computer from *The Tomorrow People*? Oh, hang on, there's that character from *Recall UNIT*, who was a *Doctor Who* fan... probably him, then.

TIME AND RELATIVE DIMENSION(S) IN SPACE: Yes, we know it was originally 'Dimension' singular – but come on, it's been 'Dimensions' for four decades now, it makes more sense that way, and only the most pedantic git who still thinks the first story is called '100,000BC' would claim otherwise. Even after 'Dimension' singular was re-established in 'Rose', the improved plural version quickly slipped into the official *Doctor Who Fun Fax* to confuse a new generation, so why bother? And while we're on the subject – look, now that the first three stories are out on DVD under their long-accepted names, can we finally stop that other nonsense, too? A *DWM* Archive on 'The Mutants', for feck's sake? Don't be so silly!

TIME RAM: There's a person who goes on the net and makes up species of Gallifreyan flora and fauna (that's plants and animals, American readers). Many dismiss her as a mentalist for having this innocent hobby. But we're with her, and in support we've made up the above beast, which produces multi-coloured wool for knitting long scarves.

TIME WAR: Epoch-spanning conflagration in which the Doctor's people were destroyed. But if only a single Time Lord had thought to flip open his TARDIS console and unleash the vortex upon the Dalek hordes, perhaps sacrificing one body in the process, things could have been so different.

The Doctor, too, could make much smarter use of his miracle machine. Then, we could dispense with the TV series altogether, as the Tardisodes would be more than long enough to relate his adventures. 'Doctor, look, Slitheens!' (Flip) 'Hurrah, they've all turned into eggs.' 'Oh no, Cybermen!' (Flip) 'Phew, they've regressed to their human forms. Where to next?' 'Help, Doctor, it's a robot version of Anne Robinson.' (Flip) 'Oh crap, now it's the real one!' 'Oops, Rose has been killed and the universe wiped out.' (Flip) 'That's better – lost a regeneration that time, though.'

TIN DOGS: With K9 being such a fantastic character – oh, of course he is, stop being so mature – you'd think there'd be a plethora of cute robot dogs lolloping about, sniffing aliens' bottoms in myriad SF shows, but sadly it isn't the case. There was Muffy in 'classic' *Battlestar Galactica*; it was a mechanical version of a daggit, which is a sort of space dog, so it counts. Although it loses a few points on the canine credentials scale by being played by a chimp in a suit, rather than being a complex automaton like the BBC's K9 prop.

Unfortunately, a rebooted equivalent of Muffy is one of the few characters absent from new *Galactica* and the series is all the poorer for it. There was also the magnificent Preston from *Wallace and Gromit in A Close Shave*, and we think we know where co-writer Bob Baker found inspiration for that character – yes indeed, it was *The Terminator*. The only other TV metal mutt we can bring to mind without doing any actual research is the particularly daft-looking Mister Pants from *Cleopatra 2525*, who could speak and was rocket-powered, though his primary field of expertise was playing fetch. Now that Sony has put down their Aibos, robot dogs are more out of vogue than ever. So let's hope Jetix eventually make that mega-budget *K9* series and do a brilliant job while they're at it. But we suspect they might not.

'TOMB OF THE CYBERMEN, THE' – THE AUDIO TAPES: Oh dear, what a shame for BBC Audio that this story was returned to the archives and rush-released just after they'd got Jon Pertwee to record linking narration for the soundtrack. Undeterred by the fact that their tape was now utterly pointless, they released it anyway. And, undeterred by thoughts of completism and the rather nice cover, we didn't buy it. Well, one of us didn't...

But hold on, what's this? A decade and a half later, and it's out again, on CD?! Who do they expect to buy it this time? Blind people? No need, as they can just as easily listen to the pristine soundtrack on the DVD, which has the added bonus of a commentary. People who like to listen to stuff in their cars? OK, but again they could watch the DVD before they go out, taking advantage of the pictures that come with it, then find something else for their journey. With Big Finish's output of almost one release per day, they're unlikely to be short of options. Or they could put on the radio – as long as Chris Moyles isn't on it, that's fine. No, the only people who'll buy this are those sad completists again, who are probably keeping their fingers crossed for an MP3 version next.*

TOP TRUMPS: No, not the Slitheen, we mean the card game. At last, *Doctor Who* has its own official set, with the Daleks in it and everything. And they give Captain Jack a 'courage' rating of 69, which is surely inten-

---

* And now 'The Ark' too, with more on the way. Are we supposed to just forget we could be looking at a real live elephant? And the Monoids really do have to be seen to be believed.

tional. But... but... it just isn't the same without all those historical figures – though we do get Madame Pompadour.

In fact, what's the point of the game at all if you can't play Heroes versus Monsters? Well, OK, you could, but the monsters would walk it cos there's more of them and you could just keep picking Monster Rating and Darkness as your categories. Better that, we suppose, than having the Doctor defeat the Daleks by being, er, taller than they are. But surely the balance could have been tipped just by changing the stats on the TARDIS card. In keeping with the TV episodes, you should be able to throw it down, destroy your opponent's entire hand and claim victory.

TOPLESS PHOTOS OF COMPANIONS IN *DWM*: Flipping heck, you wait twenty-seven years for one of these to appear, and it's bleedin' Mickey! With his underpants showing and everything. Typical!

***TOTALLY DOCTOR WHO*:** Call us disloyal, but we're totally forced to ask – was the world totally gagging for another behind-the-scenes-on-*Doctor-Who* show? Was *Confidential* not enough? Did no one notice that *Blue Peter* was totally covering the series every week anyway? And this on top of *Torchwood*, *The Sarah Jane Adventures*, Tardisodes, podcasts, *Project Who*, BBC Radio Wales's *Back in Time* series and mentions on every other show going... Isn't this getting totally out of hand? The reason the new *Doctor Who* made it so big is because it was totally different – like nothing made for British television in, ooh, years. Same reason *Big Brother* totally took off in a way its million or so imitators can only dream about. The way to repeat that success is to produce something similarly distinctive – not to keep totally flogging the same idea. And so – though, a few years ago, we'd never have thought we'd have to say this – we totally send out this appeal to BBC executives: FOR GOD'S SAKE, PLEASE, *MAKE SOMETHING ELSE*!!!

TOWER BRIDGE: Location of a real-life showdown between armed police and a Dalek, when the latter was seen approaching the Houses of Parliament in March 2005. The Dalek, of course, contained nothing more harmful than a *Doctor Who* fan filming a video. Still, when it comes to alien threats to our elected representatives, we suppose you can't be too careful.

TV60 AWARDS: Gongs handed out to the best-ever BBC shows and stars to celebrate the corporation's sixtieth anniversary in 1996. The nominees were voted for by the public, which led to most of the winners being new programmes currently in the spotlight, as the organisers had no doubt hoped. There was one big exception, though: *Doctor Who* was a late addition to the nominees, apparently at the insistence of Verity Lambert, as back then the BBC weren't too keen on owning up to ever having made it.

And so a nation, not to mention the expectant cast of *EastEnders*, watched in horror as the award for Favourite Popular Drama was collected by Peter Davison and Sylvester McCoy. The *'Stenders* lot later cast aspersions on the result, and the rumour that the *'Doctor Who* Fan Club' (sic) had frigged the system even made it onto the satirical quiz show *Have I Got News For You?*. It couldn't have been true, though – as even if *Celestial Toyroom* had urged such a campaign, it would surely have done so a month after the event. *Doctor Who*'s highlights were represented by that hoary old sequence of regeneration clips, but it could have been worse. Imagine if there'd been a tied vote, and the pinnacle of six decades of BBC drama had been a scene from 'Dimensions in Time'...

TEN **Pointless Poll Victories**

1. *Doctor Who* came ninth out of *The 100 Greatest TV Shows* in March 2001, though Channel 4 couldn't resist a dig at the JNT era by repeating that line we don't talk about from a certain Mark Gatiss/ David Walliams sketch.

2. Two months later, the Doctor himself scored an even more impressive sixth in *The 100 Greatest TV Characters*. So, obviously, his show was just dragging him down.

3. Ninth again, in C4's *100 Greatest Kids' TV Shows*, 2005, just behind *Scooby-Doo*, which perhaps explains why Russell T is so keen to emulate the latter. But hang on, how can *Doctor Who* be the ninth best kids' show and the ninth best TV show full stop? Unless the top eight in that first poll were all kids' shows, which would make sense.

4. As cheap schedule-fillers go, C4's *Top Ten* series made a refreshing change from their completely dissimilar *100 Greatest* format – and *Doctor Who*'s own Davros made it all the way to number eight in their *TV Villains* rundown of 2001, nudging ahead of *Brookside*'s Barry Grant.

5. Hard to imagine now, but just a few years ago you didn't need to be Joss Whedon to win the votes of *SFX* readers. And so it was that the Doctor got to be their Greatest Science-Fiction Character in 2003.

6. The British Association for the Advancement of Science conducted their poll to find the Top Screen Scientist alongside the BBC Cult site, so we might perhaps expect some voting bias. Nevertheless, the Doctor was beaten down to third place by Mr Spock in second and, with over twice the Vulcan's votes, Doctor Bunsen Honeydew and Beaker in first. But hang on, there are two of them – is that allowed?

7. We knew we wouldn't get away from Channel 4 for long, and indeed the bottom of their barrel was scraped by *100 Greatest Websearches* in 2006. *Doctor Who* was placed, but ironically no number of web searches will furnish us with the details.

8. No less than two mentions, though, in 2003's *100 Greatest Scary Moments* – the first appearance of a Dalek plunger at 39, with the theme tune itself at 54. Better than it looks, actually, as most of the higher entries were big-budget horror movies, with only *The X-Files* and, er, *Coronation Street* managing scarier small-screen moments. Though the presence of *Carry on Screaming* at number 30 is a bit perplexing.

9. Never a channel to let an inexpensive bandwagon roll by, Five produced *The Most Shameful TV Moments Ever* in 2005, a show that deserved a high placement in the rundown itself. And they had the cheek to put the Kandyman at number 24! Don't they recognise fine craftsmanship when they see it?

10. Finally, *100 Greatest British Television Programmes* was a list compiled by the BFI in 2000 from a poll of industry professionals. *Doctor Who* came third, after *Fawlty Towers* and *Cathy Come Home*, which... actually, that's pretty darn impressive.

- .— .- - ...: BBCi's special secret message to *Doctor Who* fans, delivered on their Geocomtex website after the transmission of 'Dalek'. We suspect an internal joke gone wrong, as the code was very quickly rewritten to read 'Bad Wolf'.

'TWIN DILEMMA, THE': The Sixth Doctor's debut extravaganza, honoured by Woolworth's as a video release (remember them?) unique to their stores. Woolies' original choice was 'The Aztecs', but they rejected it because they felt fans would prefer a colour story to a black and white one. However, such ignorance was no excuse for *TV Zone*, who boasted that they'd delayed 'The Ice Warriors' by several years and had it replaced by 'The Mark of the Rani', by simply phoning the BBC and reminding them that two episodes of the earlier story are missing. Thanks, guys!

'TWO DOCTORS, THE': Pointless and generally unwanted extra feature on the otherwise superb DVD release of 'A Fix With Sontarans'.

TYLER, JACKIE: The tenth scariest monster in new *Doctor Who*, according to *Doctor Who Adventures* – who also placed an inert Cyber-head at #2. Blimey, you wouldn't find us desperately padding out a Top Ten list like that.* We wouldn't have forgotten the Sycorax or the Nestene Consciousness for a start.

TYLER, ROSE: Russell T's greatest con trick. How on earth has he brainwashed even long-term fans into thinking she's anything but a bog-standard companion by any other name? Not that we're complaining – Rose is exactly what the series needed – we're just sick of reading how wonderful and different she is when, in her first year in particular, she resurrected the Daleks, almost destroyed the time stream and spent much of the intervening time being captured and rescued like every other companion ever. After hints about a *Buffy*-type sidekick, and with such strong female fantasy leads as Xena and Sydney Bristow having come along to kick the genre's ass since 1989, we expected a bit more. But then, Russell's masterstroke has been in presenting Rose alongside a succession of even less effectual blokes – among them Mickey, Adam and, let's face it, the Ninth Doctor.

---

* Though, having now seen Jackie's scary jug handles on Cyber-Earth, maybe they had a point.

TEN Reasons Why Rose is Nowt Special

1. She's not as hard as Leela.

2. She's not as intelligent as Romana.

3. She's not as common as Dodo.

4. She's not as elegantly-attired as Adric.

5. She's not as cute as Zoe.

6. She's not as feisty as Ace.

7. She's not as gobby as Tegan.

8. She's not as pretty as Polly.

9. She's not as unearthly as Susan.

10. She's not as well-endowed as Peri.

U

UNAUTHORIZED BUT VERY, VERY SEXY: Unusual claim of the first *I, Who* book from Sidewinder Press, presented above a photograph of a snogging couple. We're not sure what's so sexy about synopses of *Doctor Who* novels – unless they mean all those carefully itemised 'Ass-Whuppings' or... What's that? Sidewinder and Mad Norwegian are one and the same? Really? Er, how do we get out of this one, then? Wait, hang on, this ought to do it... :-) There, sorted. Phew!

UNBOUND: To celebrate the fortieth anniversary, Big Finish brought out a range of audios featuring alternative Doctors. This gave us the chance to hear a Doctor that was prepared to commit murder, one that was a writer in a universe where *Doctor Who* was never made but would have written it if it had been (or something like that), one that was evil (the Valeyard, actually), and, the most unacceptable of the lot, one that was female. Yuk!

However, the two most popular were played by Geoffrey Bayldon and David Warner, and not so coincidentally were the closest to the established character. Well, duh!

TEN   Alternative Doctors

1. Geoffrey Bayldon. He claimed on the commentary for *Catweazle* that he was offered the role of the First Doctor back in 1963. It must have been a psychic premonition of his getting the Big Finish gig, as he isn't one of the usual suspects named by Verity Lambert et al.

2. Richard E Grant. Who else thought Richard E would make an excellent Doctor only to change their opinion completely after 'Scream of the Shalka'? Though he didn't seem too bad in 'The Curse of Fatal Death', so perhaps he's really an acting genius and decided that portraying the Doctor as a two-dimensional character was the way to go in a cartoon.

3. Arabella Weir. Anyone catch *Posh Nosh*, the spoof cookery show with Arabella and Richard E? It was almost like watching some bizarre parallel universe version of 'The Two Doctors' – only better written, obviously.

4. Peter Cushing. According to *DWM*'s definitive (apart from all the mistakes) episode guide in the late eighties, Peter the Great played the 'title role' in the film *Daleks – Invasion Earth 2150 AD*. He also starred as 'Doctor Who' in two other movies – though in *At the Earth's Core*, the character went under the pseudonym of Dr Abner Perry.

5. Sir Derek Jacobi. A glance at his CV makes it look like this accomplished actor is in the unique position of having played both the Doctor and his arch-enemy the Master. But the fact that he actually played a writer called Martin who dreamt of being the Doctor and a robot Master means he's played neither. Dunno why we put him on the list at all, really.

6. Jim Broadbent. He's virtually made a career out of playing unofficial Doctors. Well, he's done it twice, anyway.

7. Lily Savage. In the days when Paul O'Grady made his living dressing up as an old slapper, he too starred in a *Doctor Who-*

based comedy sketch, accompanied by busty but thick page three stunna Gayle Tuesday. We're not sure what to think about this one, though – it's just too confusing trying to work out if it counts as a female Doctor or not.

8. David Collings. At last we understand how Tegan, Nyssa and the Brigadier could have mistaken Mawdryn for the not-at-all-similar-and-wearing-different-clothes-anyway Fifth Doctor: they must have encountered David's Unbound incarnation in an unseen adventure. Even so, the shredded wheat on his bonce should have been a giveaway. After all, just a couple of stories earlier, the girls had had no trouble telling the near-identical Omega from their travelling companion thanks to a smattering of Rice Krispies on his face.

9. Trevor Martin. Big Finish has employed him, so why they haven't taken the opportunity to produce an audio version of *Doctor Who and the Daleks in Seven Keys to Doomsday*, we don't know.

10. Christopher Eccleston. The oddest Unbound incarnation to date: a Doctor who talks and dresses like a normal bloke from Salford, never saves the day and probably fancies his... oh. Apparently, he was a proper one.

UNDERPANTS: Items of clothing that, according to 'The Seeds of Death', would in future be worn on the outside in Superman-like fashion. Phew, good job that prediction's not come true yet – or else being a *Doctor Who* fan with a pair of Tom Baker undies would just be embarrassing.

UNIT: United Nations Intelligence Taskforce. At least it used to be, until the real-life UN kicked up a fuss about... well, we're not sure what, exactly. It's not like the British government or the Royal Family complained about being linked with Torchwood – and can you imagine if the US government or the CIA whinged about every piece of fiction that implicated them in a conspiracy theory? What's so harmful about being said to be out there protecting us from Sycorax and Slitheen, anyway? Good to know, though, that the UN have presumably ended all wars, corruption and poverty in their member states and can waste their time on such trivia.

UNIT BASE: Enigmatic sign that appeared on Salford's main road, the Crescent, during the writing of this book. Eventually, we gave in and followed it, wondering if perhaps the alien-fighting organisation from TV's *Doctor Who* was real after all, and had set up a secret but as always well-signposted HQ in our neck of the woods. Sadly, it turned out to be to do with some production company making a TV programme, with no spaceships in it or anything. Hardly worth mentioning, then.

UNIT SECURITY CODE RED: You knew it was coming, don't pretend you didn't. A far more fiendish and complex cipher than the simple substitution code that was its green counterpart (and if you haven't translated that entry in Volume 1 yet, you obviously don't know your ARSE from your ELBO); so much so that even the invaluable UNIT codebook got its sample message wrong. But then, *Doctor Who Weekly* also mixed up its Green and Red messages the first two times it used 'em – doh! So, only the saddest of the sad need bother with the following: Rdxr uvyilagmn srcrtdnltmdra sydarcb eli lalpr lrkmywprid, taiv ddxr Apgadrn vnmia ilbb. Egiv sal, Imgadrnwcgi 'Sk' gya adxqgndrv. Ytln, bdmnirv ulmd tdl tjr hg ajyd tlb sg nvrma ore Tpgtxyig tyi hdxr eriv, avyvi'd nyd! Sdxgiza wgiuqgu edl Rjrniyr Tbyaxildra' Rtlpwcrdrcu Ymarcraa Hqrjaydr abln rnrtgwwyis ddxr epyaayis rqngwwrn.

UNIVERSE FOUR: Location of the planet Quinnis, once visited by the First Doctor and Susan apparently. Either the writer hadn't been paying attention to *The Sky at Night* or this is an early example of the TARDIS being able to traverse the multiverse, thus validating comments made years later in 'The Age of Steel'. In fact, it's probably both.

UNREQUITED LOVE: Hang on a mo, let's make sure we've got this right: Sarah Jane didn't just want to be friends with the Doctor, she wanted to play hide the Alpha Centauri with him too? Because that's the impression given in 'School Reunion'. And if only Sarah had made a lunge for the Fifth Doctor's sticky wicket in 'The Five Doctors', they wouldn't have had to write the anniversary story out of continuity to make that point. There are a couple of ways to explain Sarah's forgetfulness regarding her visit to the Death Zone: either the Time Lords erased her memory, or it was a knock-on effect from that Time War thing we know so little about. A further possibility is that she made the whole crush thing up, and only wants to get a grip of the Doctor now that he looks like Casanova.

UP THE ARSE CORNER: Regular column (oo-er) in once-very-funny adult comic *Viz*, which has twice featured well-known *Doctor Who* photos: the first of the Northern Doctor being taken from behind by an Auton, the second of the Fourth Doctor getting similar treatment from a 'Revenge' Cyberman.

Viz has often featured *Who*-related foolery; apart from *Doctor Poo* (see list accompanying **LE DOCTEUR OMEGA**), they also scored what was sort of the first ever comic book appearance of the Northern Doctor, in their *Suicidal Syd* strip. Hoping as always to get himself killed, Syd went along to the filming of the new series, found some interested bystanders and shouted out '*Doctor Who* fans are a bunch of puffs!' But the fans just agreed that he had a point, and went off to discuss the matter on the Internet.

VENOM GRUBS: Enforcers of the death penalty on Raxacoricofalla-patorious, and presumably – given a mention of the Isop Galaxy in the following episode – the same creatures the Doctor encountered on the planet Vortis. But hang on, weren't they called Larva Guns on screen? A sure sign, then, that the Welsh series is set in the non-canonical universe of *Doctor Who and the Zarbi*, *TV Comic* and the Peter Cushing films – that strange place where the character really is called Dr Who.

VERVOIDS: Well, what a kettle of Fish People we opened up when, last time out, we suggested that these monsters looked a bit rude. Seems that, while everyone agrees they resemble a body part of a private nature, there's some dispute as to which it might be. Frankly, we don't understand those fans who, when they look at the Sixth Doctor's greatest enemies, see something not dissimilar to Alpha Centauri staring back at them; we had something more... feminine in mind.

But to complicate things further, there's Bonnie Langford's assertion that she and her fellow actors thought the Vervoids looked like 'bottoms'. Obviously, there's something deep and psychological going on here. In fact, could it be that, quite by accident, the Vervoid's head is the perfect 3-D equivalent of a Rorschach inkblot test? If so, it could well be used as such by psychoanalysts in the future – though of course, it'll be the people who describe the proffered shape as 'a monster from the 1986 series of the popular TV series *Doctor Who*' who'll be first in line for the padded cells.

VIDFART: Early name for the VidFIRE process, and the one by which we still like to think of it. VidFART is used in the restoration of old episodes, to – if we may get as technical as we can here – make them look good. Nothing to complain about there, you might think – if you didn't know *Doctor Who* fans at all. Some would rather have kept the old, grainy film prints – because, it turns out, those early classics are much more impressive when you can't see them properly. Remember when Patrick Troughton's TARDIS looked like it had roundels, not just tatty roundel-patterned wallpaper? And don't get us started on those Optera costumes... Fortunately, for anyone concerned that an increase in picture clarity means a drop in the atmosphere of a production, we have this suggestion: Drape a net curtain over your TV screen, and watch it with sunglasses on. There, good as old.

VIRGIN RAIL: Blimey, they only went and named one of their trains *Doctor Who*! It's one of their Voyager fleet – nothing to do with *Star Trek*, apparently, but everything to do with famous explorers. Cue jokes about the Doctor's time-keeping, his vehicle being historically under-funded, cancellation crises, Peri's buffers, etc.

VOICE, THE NATION'S FAVOURITE: Poll conducted by the *Radio Times*, and won by the rich tones of Tom Baker – though some people probably meant to vote for Jon Culshaw. Interestingly enough, a former Doctor had the favourite female voice too. Joanna Lumley, that is – who did you think we meant, Colin Baker? With all that vocal talent in the *Who* world, someone should really make audio adventures. Oh, wait a minute, someone is. Just not with Tom Baker or Joanna Lumley.

VULPANA: It's a science-fiction cliché, of course, to name your world after the Latin genus name for the type of creatures that live there. Thankfully, *Doctor Who* has succumbed less often than you might imagine. A shame, then, that its planet of werewolves was mistaken for a planet of foxes. Or perhaps it was a cunning deception on the Vulpanans' part, to lure unwary linguists into their claws. Come to think of it, that Mags was a bit of a fox...

WALES: Where *Doctor Who* is now made. For the benefit of geographically naïve American readers, Wales is a small county in England. There is a Welsh language of sorts, but it is primarily used for insulting English tourists. Famous Welshies include Manchester United footballer Ryan Giggs, Glynn out of *Big Brother* and Superted. Before becoming a droid, Anne Robinson was best known for disliking the Welsh.

WALKIE TALKIES: Constructed in the forms of the Ninth Doctor and a Slitheen, these toys are a small step up from two baked bean cans connected by a piece of string. Not only can they be used for the purposes of communication, they can be played with like regular action figures. The likeness of the Doctor is fairly accurate, although the ears are not to scale, presumably to save costs on plastic. This is in marked contrast to the Denys Fisher Leela doll which, you'll no doubt recall, had its lovely lady lumps expanded to the dimensions of a *Big Brother* contestant's. The Slitheen is very good too (well, only in the sense that it looks like one off the telly), though we feel the manufacturers missed an opportunity for added authenticity by placing the speaker in its chest rather than its arse.

WALLINGER, MARK: A renowned contemporary artist, we're told, with a bit of a TARDIS fetish. In 2001, he unveiled the fruits of a year-long residency at the Oxford University Museum of Natural History: an installation comprising two police boxes, one outside the building, one inside. The concept, apparently, was that as you couldn't see both at once, you couldn't prove they weren't the same box, having slipped through the time/space vortex ahead of you – a flawed notion, we find, in this age of camera phones.

But what astounds us is that Wallinger didn't build the things himself, he bought them from This Planet Earth! Makes you wonder what he did for the other 364 and a half days of the year, doesn't it? 'But is it art?' asked everyone. Well, we aren't schooled in this area, and may lack the specialised vocabulary to do justice to a detailed critique, but we would like to take a stab at answering that question: No, it isn't. However, a couple of years later, Wallinger did build a TARDIS of his very own, with mirrored panels to give the illusion that it was in mid-dematerialisation. It was displayed in the Whitechapel Gallery – and it looked great!

'WE WANT MUFFIN': Fifties TV presenter Annette Mills' sung plea in 'The Idiot's Lantern'. Punch line removed for being far too obvious.

'WEIRDO STALKERS': The *Daily Star*'s insulting label for fans who turn up in Cardiff to watch filming of the new series. Far be it from us to defend any so-called weirdoes – but surely the urge to witness the creation of a piece of television history is perfectly understandable and acceptable. Hence the fact that the *Daily Star* presumably sent journalists there to record the event for their 'weirdo' readers.

WELSH SERIES WITH THE TAXICAB LOGO, THE: Did you notice how we kept ourselves in check and refrained from using this term throughout the book? It really was a challenge!

WEREWOLF: Concluding our pedantic inventory of Welsh *Doctor Who* monsters that look quite like other things, we draw your attention to CGI werewolves in *Van Helsing*, *Underworld*, *Cursed*, etc., take your pick. Having said that, there's no denying the *Doctor Who* one was extremely well-designed and realised – and on a TV budget too. Certainly a lot better than the one in *Harry Potter and the Prisoner of Azkhaban*! For a battle that could easily match that between Daleks and Cybermen, perhaps this Space Wolf could return to become the Space Pig's greatest enemy, particularly if the latter were to build some kind of dwelling.

'WE'VE EVEN GOT A BIT OF A LOVE LIFE': Something to bear in mind when laying a paving stone: Only the front half of Ursula's head protruded from the concrete, so presumably there's only so far Elton could have got without a painful stubbing incident[*]. Or maybe we

---

[*] That Amazon-exclusive Cyber-head Series Two DVD should probably come with a warning, for certain fans.

should see this as proof that what you told the kids was true: they were just talking about kissing!

WHAT AM I DOING HERE?: Regular feature in the BBC staff magazine *Ariel*, in which a member of the corporation's staff talks about their job. Except that, one week in May 2006, they interviewed fictional character John Lumic of Cybus Industries instead. On his world, the piece revealed, Lumic abolished the BBC to make his own Cybusnet the sole global information provider. He also talked extensively about his love of zeppelins, his Sleep Replacement System and his need for immortality, and revealed that he spent most of his childhood above the coast of New Germany, inventing.

On the subject of the Cybermen, he noted that early models were allergic to gold and that their original name, picked by focus groups, was Cybusmen. Lumic was interviewed by Tom MacRae 'prior to his conversion to become CyberController'. So, in a sense, his wisdom was coming to us... sorry, we can't resist it... FROM BEYOND THE GRAVE!!!

WHO: Fictional organisation established in Chris Claremont's UK-based *X-Men* spin-off comic *Excalibur* in 1989. The Weird Happenings Organisation was headed up by a Brigadier Alysande Stuart, with scientific advice provided by her twin brother Alistaire. A complete rip-off, you might feel[*] – but hang on, the organisation's headquarters was in the Tower of London. And in the new *Doctor Who*, UNIT are based in the Tower too. So, it's a case of *Who*'s copying WHO?!

WHOGRAPHS: Not a real word at all, but rather one made up by taking the word *Who* from *Doctor Who* and combining it with the word autographs. What confuses us about this recent Telos release – for the most part, a book of empty pages – is that it contains replica signatures of departed *Who* luminaries on its inside covers. Why so defeatist? Granted, there's little chance of our getting the originals now – but still, it's not inconceivable that Derek Acorah might do a convention some day, is it?

WHOISDOCTORWHO.CO.UK: Spitting image of Clive's site, which could be found by tapping 'Doctor blue box' into Google just as Rose did

---

[*] Though this was subtle, compared to appearances by a Brigadier Lethbridge-Stewart and a Sergeant-Major Benton, helping to defend Edinburgh from the Juggernaut, in a Claremont-scripted issue of *Uncanny X-Men* two years earlier. More recently, the same writer established that the Fantastic Four had a dimensionally transcendental police box in their back garden – a gift to Reed Richards from 'that weird "Doctor" friend of his' – though the artist obviously didn't know what a police box was and drew a classic red telephone box instead. Still, an easy mistake to make.

(though surely, we feel, in a world where there aren't a billion *Doctor Who*-related web pages, she should have had to wade through a ton of medical porn first?).

Alas, BBCi were beaten to the punch by a fan site, which had two big advantages: (1) It didn't have the bloody disclaimer and the giveaway links to BBC pages; and (2) You could contact Clive with any info. We e-mailed to say we'd seen the bloke in his photo in an Eccles pub, watching a United match, but just got an auto-reply message to say that Clive would be in touch. Presumably this was because he was dead, having – by a remarkable coincidence – gone to the same shopping arcade as Rose's mum and the Autons.

WHONIVERSE: Term used to describe the place where *Doctor Who* adventures occur (no, not London). It is not, erm, universally popular among fans because although it is a logical amalgamation of the words *Who* and universe, it does sound very silly indeed. The Whoniverse is obviously parallel to our own universe as evidenced by the bizarre happenings there, such as a spaceships appearing in the skies and Shayne Warne some day having enough material to fill a Greatest Hits album.

WHO-RU: Hilariously titled quiz segment of *Totally Doctor Who*, the producers of which thought it'd be a good idea to snatch away the most totally prized possessions of its young contestants should they lose. The format was abandoned after Noel Clarke totally tried his best to let the first kid win but ended up owning her home-made dragon (he gave it back to her, along with the T-shirt she had totally failed to earn, so what was the point?). There's still the odd hiccup, though. Cassandra *did* play Toxic on her jukebox as well as Tainted Love, so it's totally just as well that the girl who lost out there didn't have to hand over her Playstation or something.

WHO'S BLAKE: Both Tom Baker and Blake himself, Gareth Thomas, thought it would be a fun visual joke for their respective space-travelling characters to bump into each other during an adventure, let on, and then continue about their business. Sadly, this unprecedented BBC seventies sci-fi crossover was never to take place. Indeed, unlike some of his *Liberator* crewmates, Thomas has never appeared in televised *Doctor Who* – though he has done a couple of Big Finish audios, which almost counts. Come to think of it, if there had been a *Doctor Who/ Blake's 7* crossover, we'd have preferred it to feature Soolin anyway!

TEN
Cult TV Favourites Who've Never Appeared in (TV) *Doctor Who*

1. Nicholas Young. An obvious choice, we'd have thought, as *The Tomorrow People* was ITV's answer to *Doctor Who*. Yeah, snigger, of course it was. But anyone who's ever seen the DVDs of the series will know it's worth casting Mr Young in any show anyway, just so he'll be eligible to appear on the subsequent DVD commentary.

2. Annette Andre. She was probably too busy appearing in *Randall and Hopkirk (Deceased)*, *The Baron*, *The Saint*, *Return of the Saint*, *The Avengers*, *The New Avengers*, *Adam Adamant Lives!*, *The Prisoner*, *The Persuaders!*, and *Prisoner: Cell Block H*.

3. Ed Bishop. Too late now...

4. Michael Mackenzie. Whatever did happen to that *Ace of Wands* DVD set?

5. Gerald Harper. He worked with both Sidney Newman and Verity Lambert on *Adam Adamant Lives!*, so it's not like he didn't have the right contacts.

6. Keeley Hawes. Hot actress from *Spooks*, reportedly high on the shortlist of possible companions for the Eccleston series. She didn't get the job (obviously), and we do like Billie, but there's still some lingering disappointment.

7. Tony Gardner. Though appearing as Brian in *My Parents are Aliens* means he already plays the most eccentric alien on British TV.

8. Diana Rigg. She's only done Bond and *The Avengers* up to now, so Honor Blackman is winning 3-2.

9. Roger Moore. Not that he's ever been that hard up for work, though.

10. Zoe Tapper. The prettiest and most talented of the *Hex* cast – one to bear in mind for the future, maybe?

'WHO'S THE DALEK ON THE STAIRCASE?': Comedy insult delivered by Anne Robinson – who really ought to have known better – on the 14/3/06 edition of *The Weakest Link*. Will we never get through to these people?

WHOSPY: BBCi feature that tantalises us with images from the filming of upcoming episodes. Unfortunately, the *Doctor Who* production office are a tad secretive, so all we get to see are make-up bags, bits of carpet, blurry paperwork, the backs of scenery flats and, in one thrilling instalment, the keys to the production office. (Is it just us, or could someone have used this to make a copy of said keys, sneak into the office and steal last year's scripts? No wonder they had to switch buildings!) This was extravagant, though, compared to what the official magazine got. *DWM* had to promote the first episodes of the brand new series with, er, no photos at all – unlike all the unofficial magazines and newspapers, which ran candid shots of Daleks, other monsters and Eccleston in 'costume'. And in the end, what was it all for? Our tellies were so full of clips of 'Rose' the week before it aired, the only way to enjoy it spoiler-free was to... well, to watch the copy that leaked out early on the Internet, quite frankly. The Beeb kicked up a predictable fuss about that, calling it 'a serious breach of copyright' – but it gave them another excuse to plug their expensive new show on the news, so where was the harm?

NINE Most Exasperating Spoilers for New *Doctor Who* (and One That Wasn't)

1. Rose goes into the TARDIS. Rose comes out of the TARDIS, runs around it, goes back in... and the writing and direction of that sequence taunt us, holding off the Big Reveal until the perfect moment. Except... They filmed all the trailers on the bloody console room set, so what was the point?

2. The return of the Daleks in 'Bad Wolf'. The good news is, it remained an end-of-episode surprise as planned. The bad news

is, thanks to an over-zealous 'Throw Forward' (see '**NEXT TIME...**'), the episode was 'Boom Town'.

3. That 'secret' regeneration, kept for all of, ooh, one day after the series began. Just imagine what that would have been like, had someone not blabbed.

4. So, why were all the publicity shots of Sarah Jane and K9 taken with the 'new' model from the end of 'School Reunion'? Made it pretty obvious that, when the knackered one got blown up, it wasn't quite the end.

5. And then there were those photos in the *Radio Times*, showing us just how the Doctor would save the day in 'The Girl in the Fireplace', with Alison Graham mentioning it in her column to make sure we hadn't missed it. Even Steven Moffat felt compelled to warn *Outpost Gallifrey* posters not to open those pages before the big day.

6. But if we felt let down by *RT*, how much worse to learn from *DWM* of all places that 'The Age of Steel' would be Mickey's last episode. Thanks, guys!

7. So, this fan wins a charity auction and gets a day on the *Doctor Who* set. Only no one thinks to mention that everything he sees is top secret. Cue one gushing Internet review of the experience, containing the words 'Daleks' and 'Cybermen'. Cue various people hitting various roofs. Thing is, we might have written the whole thing off as guesswork or a joke had that reaction not pretty much confirmed it.

8. With that in mind, then, how careless was it to take to the BAFTAs stage with a lovely Black Dalek that hadn't yet been seen on screen? And if you didn't catch that – ooh, look, there's a familiar extermination effect in the 'Throw Forward' for 'Army of Ghosts'. One that had no right being in there anyway, as it was actually from 'Doomsday'! As was the shot of Mickey and Pete Tyler that was grabbed and displayed on a thousand Internet pages...

9. OK, so they eventually just told us about the Cybermen's return in 'Army of Ghosts'. But not before they'd dished out photos of a black-jugged Cyber-Leader to all and sundry. 'Hmm,' we all

thought after his no-show in both 'Rise of the Cybermen' and 'The Age of Steel', 'wonder when we'll see him?'

10. And the one that wasn't: That blank space on the *Radio Times* giveaway poster with the caption 'The Tenth Doctor Regenerates'. Ooh, the speculation that caused before the sticker arrived the following week to reveal a simple case of careless wording.

WIRE, THE: First the gaseous entities the Gelth, then the electrical Wire. Maybe Mark Gatiss is getting back at the power suppliers for their over-the-top utility bills. If his next monster is composed entirely of H2O, we'll know his water rates were a bit excessive too.

Um, er... OK, so **X-RANI AND THE UGLY MUTANTS** it is, then: On the planet Xethra, Romana is scared and sickened by the sight of some ugly people. She and the Doctor run round for a bit trying to catch one, and encounter the beautiful X-Rani.

X-Rani reveals that the ugly mutants were exiled here from Ethra (hmm, we suspect an anagram there), while anyone with disabilities was sent to Yethra. She's in charge of the mutants, and has been keeping them busy by controlling their minds and forcing them to fight. X-Rani has to wear a veil, because the mutants can't bear her beauty – but at least she's been told that, once they're all dead, she can go home. Recently, however, the Controller of Ethra has cut off supplies of the essential foodstuff bavita, so X-Rani uses a strange ability on the Doctor, giving him a first degree mutation and promising to cure it only if he helps her.

The Doctor and X-Rani leave Romana behind to look after the mutants, while they travel to Ethra. The Controller is in a guarded igloo, so X-Rani uses her power on the Doctor again, making him so ugly that all the guards scream, faint or flee. The Controller and X-Rani have a mental scrap, which ends when the Doctor shoots X-Rani with a micro-laser. He has realised that the Controller was actually a prisoner, X-Rani being the one who has taken over the world and exiled its misfits. Having heard that the Doctor was on his way, she had planned to deceive him into thinking all was well (so, taking him straight to the Controller's igloo could be seen as something of an unwise move). In a final ironic twist, we learn that bavita isn't an essential foodstuff after all, though it can be used to make tea.

Hmmm, no, sorry, not a patch on 'War on Aquatica', is it? Where are the Lumidolphs, for a start?

YATES, MIKE: And here we all thought he was just a drip who wanted to get into Jo Grant's knickers. Suddenly, along come the novels, and he's a right old MARY. By which we mean, his full name is now said to be Michael Alexander Raymond Yates. Oh, and that he turns up in *Happy Endings* sporting a pink triangle, living with a man called Tom and generally acting as camp as Jo Grant's knickers.

But no, hang on, looks like the actor himself has other ideas – because, according to Richard Franklin's CD reading of his own, ahem, unpublished novel *The Killing Stone*, Yates was actually a wealthy, sophisticated James Bond-type man of action all along (a delusion previously displayed in print by Ian Marter). And his being slung out of UNIT in disgrace? A ruse, of course, to allow the good Captain to go undercover and enjoy an exciting adventure with gallstones and the Master. In fact, compared to Yates, all the men of UNIT turn out to be quite dim – though none more so than Benton, who now sounds like the illegitimate offspring of Pam Ayres and the Wurzels. Distressingly, Franklin makes the most of this second opportunity, after *Recall UNIT*, to clad the rugged sergeant in a dress. Hmm. You know, suddenly we can see Yates in Jo Grant's knickers after all...

'YIKES! HE'S ANCIENT!': *Doctor Who Adventures'* verdict on William Hartnell. Apparently, the editors find it hard to believe he was ever the First Doctor – though, due to the brevity of their articles, the reason for this disbelief is never quite made clear. They should invest in 'The

Beginning' DVD box set, as this would surely settle the matter once and for all.

'YOU NEVER F**KING KNOW THE ANSWER WHEN IT'S IMPORTANT': What the Fourth Doctor really thought of K9, albeit in a scene recorded only for the BBC's in-house Christmas video tape. We suggest he could have found even more humour in the simple but devastating observation that – wait for it – *K9 can't climb stairs!* No wonder he was eventually reduced to being a consolation prize for three successive departing companions. Though maybe we'd think more kindly if his DVD career had been managed a bit more sympathetically. Anyone enchanted by the metal mutt's sacrifice in 'School Reunion' and looking for more canine computer fun would, at the time of writing in the UK, have to make do with the first few minutes of 'The Leisure Hive', in which K9 heroically goes for a swim and blows up.

TEN Things K9 Got Up to Behind The Doctor's Back

1. Mks 1 and 2 made appearances on *Blue Peter* in character, the first to be attacked by a jealous Shep while chatting to John Noakes, the second to pass judgement on a viewer's model of himself and to sniff Goldie's bottom. Both versions claimed to be in telepathic contact with the Doctor, though they never displayed such a useful ability in the series.

2. Mk 1 escaped from Gallifrey to fly about in his own spaceship in a series of four Sparrow books. The ship was called K-NEL, which provided a brilliant but sadly overlooked opportunity for fake swearing, e.g., 'K-NEL, it's the Beasts of Vega.' 'K-NEL, it's a time trap.' 'K-NEL, it's someone who looks a bit like Omega and has the same origin story but is actually called Omegon in a cunning copyright-dodging ruse.'

3. Mk 2 enjoyed a solo comic strip outing, *K9's Finest Hour*, in ~~Doctor Who Weekly~~ – in which, alas, his shortcomings were exposed by the assassin Rolgof, who advised his robot henchmen to 'Hold his head pointing away from you so he can't shoot at you... then pick him up and take him away!'

4. This K9 also popped up on *Larry Grayson's Generation Game*, and added to the innuendo with a most uncharacteristic crack about lady dogs' entrances.

5. Having become Sarah Jane's best friend in *K9 and Company*, Mk 3 had lots more occult-lite fun in his own World annual – a rare accolade for a supporting character otherwise only afforded to the Daleks and the Jelly Babies. Of course, it was this model who returned for the new series, in which... oh my god, they killed K9. You bastards!

6. Mk 3 also teamed up with everyone's favourite Brixtonian Time Lord, Drax, and YOU to find the Doctor after he was captured by... K-NEL, it's the real Omega! See the 'Find Your Fate' book *Search for the Doctor* for the thrilling outcomes.

7. Mk 2 went gallivanting about E-Space in two BBV audios, with a woman who was most definitely not Romana, no indeedy. See **MISTRESS, THE**.

8. Mks 1 and 2 accompanied their respective mistresses in Big Finish's *Gallifrey* series, until... oh my god, they killed K9. Mk 1, that is. You bastards!

9. An unidentified model (Mk 4?) ended up on a market stall being dismantled for spare parts, until his brain was rescued by a boy called Jack and, as far as we can tell, copied onto a CD, in 'Kept Safe and Sound' – a short story by Paul Magrs in *Short Trips: Companions*.

10. And coming up, so we've been led to believe on and off for many years: a solo series first thought to be a *Captain Pugwash*-style animation but now apparently live-action with a CGI K9 – a big-eared flying one that looks like a space hopper. See also **TIN DOGS**.

YOUNG DOCTORS: Any actors out there who think they have the necessary charisma and personality to become the next Doctor had better think again if they're over the age of forty-five. In fact, just forget it, that's positively ancient and the filming schedule would be far too gruelling for someone of their advancing years. This is what Russell T seems to think, anyway. We disagree. William Hartnell was knocking on a bit during his time as the Doctor and surely his schedule was tougher still. They made the series practically all year round back then, and even had to rehearse it first.

Indeed, if Hartnell wanted so much as a day off he had to record a voiceover just so he could pretend to be invisible or something. But we suspect this argument will fall on deaf ears, and future Doctors will indeed be young, fit, virile, and ... hold on, are we missing something here?

'YOU'RE SO GAY': Offhand comment by Rose to the Doctor in 'Aliens of London', and predictably a bone of contention among online *Doctor Who* fans, who don't need much to spark them off. In a private e-mail quoted extensively on the net, Russell T Davies argued – and we agree with him – that by drawing attention to the prevalent use of the word 'gay' in this context in a family drama, he could galvanise viewers into taking a stand against it. 'Good television isn't television which makes you smile all the time and agree. If it makes you stand up and object – especially where you weren't expecting it – then that's a brilliant and powerful thing,' said the big shirt-lifter. Oh, and see **GAY AGENDA**, obviously.

ZEPPELINS: Seen floating over Great Britain in 'Rise of the Cybermen', they sort of gave the impression that, on this parallel version of Earth, the Nazis had won the war. Oh, but then there was a black President, so maybe not after all. In fact, we weren't quite sure what was supposed to have gone on; apart from Ricky, the place didn't have much of a parallel vibe to it at all. Maybe if the alternate Jackie had worn an eye-patch, or at the very least a goatee beard and moustache...

ZYGON: Highly anticipated spin-off film, mostly shot by BBV in 2002 – until, claiming not to be happy with the near-finished product, Bill Baggs himself pulled it from the schedule. Why do we care? Because *Zygon* was rumoured to be an 'adult' movie, with glimpses of bare flesh and every-thing. What would we have seen? Zygons' knobbly bits? Given their shape-changing ability, the possibilities are endless... They could have opened an agency! C'mon, Bill, don't keep this lost gem to yourself. We don't mind if it's rubbish – we're used to that – we're just curious. Surely you can see it would be a far more entertaining world in which a mucky video about Zygons exists? On which note, we seem to have come full circle, don't we?

SELECTED BIBLIOGRAPHY

How Xena Changed Our Lives: True Stories by Fans for Fans, Nikki Stafford (ed.), ECW Press, 2002.

Basil Brush Annual 1972, anon., World Distributors (Manchester) Ltd., 1971.

Essential Iron Man Vol. 2, Stan Lee, et al., Marvel Comics, 2004.

Barbara Windsor's Book of Boobs ('My boobs will give everyone hours of fun!'), anon., Hamlyn Paperbacks, 1976.

The Doctor Who Dinosaur Book (with colour poster), Terrance Dicks, W. H. Allen & Co. Ltd., 1976.

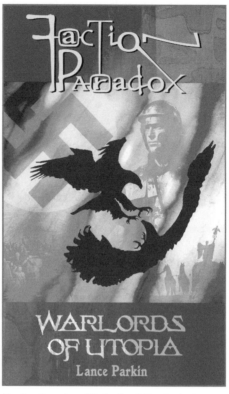

WARLORDS OF UTOPIA

Adolf Hitler, the Gaol.

In the exact centre of the island was a tower.

It was an ugly concrete stump four storeys high, a brutalist version of a medieval keep. There were tiny slits for windows. There wasn't a door. Around the tower, thorns and weeds had grown into a jungle. The tower held one prisoner.

Surrounding it was an electric fence. And the guards. Millions of strong men and women with the bodies they should have had, unmarked by armband or tattoo, allowed to grow up and grow old. Proud people, many with names like Goldberg, Cohen and Weinstein. Men and women who would never forgive. Men and women who lived in the vast, beautiful community that surrounded the tower, keeping him awake with their laughter, their music, the smell of their food, the sight of their clothes, the sound of their language and their prayers and the cries of their babies. They felt they had a duty to be here. They had always been free to leave, but few had.

On Resurrection Day itself, some had realised that as everyone who had ever lived was in the City, then *he* was here. It had taken longer to hunt him down. Few knew where he'd been found, how he'd been leading his life. Had he tried to disguise himself? Had he proclaimed his name and tried to rally supporters? It didn't matter. He had been brought here, his identity had been confirmed and he had been thrown in the tower that had been prepared for him.

Some of those living in sight of the tower had wondered if they were protecting him from the people of the City, not protecting the City from him. And it was true: the City - the glorious, colourful, polymorphous, diverse City, with uncounted races of people living side by side - was the ultimate negation of the prisoner's creed. The vast, vast majority people of the City didn't care who he was and couldn't comprehend his beliefs, let alone be swayed by his rhetoric. Individuals who'd killed, or wanted to kill, many more people than he had remained at liberty and found themselves powerless. Had imprisoning him marked out as special? Such things were argued about, but the prisoner remained in his tower.

Every day bought requests from individuals, organisations and national groupings who had come up with some way to harm him within the protocols of the City. There were also representations from his supporters, or from civil liberties groups, concerned that his imprisonment was vigilante justice or that no attempt was being made to rehabilitate him. There were historians and psychologists and journalists who wanted to interview him. There were those that just wanted to gawp at or prod the man they'd heard so much about. All of them were turned away.

One man had come here in person. An old Roman, in light armour.

The clerk, a pretty girl with dark hair and eyes, greeted him.

'Your name?'

'Marcus Americanius Scriptor.'

While she dialled up his records and waited for them to appear on her screen, she asked: 'He's after your time. You're a historian?'

'I was,' the old man said. 'May I see him?'

'The prisoner isn't allowed visitors, or to communicate with the outside world. He is allowed to read, but not to write. Oh, that's odd. Your record isn't coming up.'

'It wouldn't.' The Roman didn't elaborate.

He looked out over the city to the tower. The young woman was struck by how solemn his face was. Most people who came all the way out here were sightseers, sensation seekers. Even some of the gaolers treated the prisoner with levity. Mocking him, belittling him.

'Don't you ever want to let him loose?' he asked, finally. 'Let him wander the streets, let his words be drowned out. On another world he was an indifferent, anonymous painter.'

'It sounds like you know that for certain,' she said, before checking herself. 'To answer the question: no. He stays here.'

'I met him,' the Roman told her. 'On a number of occasions.'

She frowned.

'A long story,' he told her. 'I suppose I'm concerned that you torture yourselves by having that monster in your midst.'

The woman had heard many people say such a thing.

'Not a monster. A human being.'

'But the only human being you've locked away for all eternity.'

'The wardens have ruled that he will be freed,' she told him.

Americanius Scriptor seemed surprised. 'When?'

'First he must serve his sentence, then he will be released.'

'When?' he asked again.

'In six million lifetimes,' she told him.

Marcus Americanius Scriptor smiled.

'I'll be waiting for him,' he told her. He turned and headed back to the docks.

introducing the all-new novel...

ERASING
SHERLOCK

London: October, 1890

John Watson threw open the study door of 221-B Baker Street and crossed immediately to one of the arched windows, a terse growl cutting short the detective's cheery greeting. Drawing back the curtain a fraction, he peered down onto the street.

Holmes came up behind him and looked out over his shoulder. 'You've noticed the veiled woman, I see.'

'She followed me from Paddington Station,' the doctor hissed. 'Sat right across from me, bold as you please, in the same carriage on the train -'

'Why are you whispering? She can't hear us, you know.'

'I've no time for these games of intrigue, Holmes!'

The detective winced and poked a finger into his ear. 'Something between a whisper and roar, perhaps…'

Watson crossed his arms over his chest and glared. 'I have a practice. A wife. A child on the way.'

Holmes jerked the curtains wide and looked out. 'It's not as if I directed her to follow you,' he said. 'She's been a faithful dog on *my* heels, as well.'

Across the street, the woman inclined her head to him. The weighted veil that covered her face - temple to temple, hat-brim to chin - was impervious to any breeze that might expose her features to passersby. Something about her put him in mind of a dog, in fact, or rather a dog act in a variety show; as if she were a creature entirely unsuited to walking upright, let alone wearing a bustle. And yet the fact that she was doing it was a slap in the face: *any idiot can pretend to be human.*

Behind him, Watson sighed with gusty irritation. 'I assume she's the reason for your cryptic telegram this morning?'

'Partly. And there is also *that*.' Holmes directed the doctor's gaze to a parcel, slumped upon the dining table like an aged alley cat. 'It was here when I awoke this morning. Mrs. Hudson claims no responsibility for accepting delivery. Intriguing, yes?'

Watson limped over to a chair nearer the fire, and lowered himself into the worn seat, hat in hand and still wearing his overcoat; a sign that he did not intend to stay, which he then proceeded to emphasize. 'Well, then, perhaps we could skip past the business of you directing me to look for the clues, me failing to find them, and then, after some exposition, you revealing what's in the package before actually unwrapping it.'

'You *are* in a mood!'

'Have you heard nothing I've said, Holmes? I will not be embroiled in this, whatever it is. I'm very busy in my practice, and my wife is nearing the time of her confinement!'

'Oh. *Oh*. Of course. I'd quite forgotten your anticipation of the happy event.' The detective blinked in sudden puzzlement. 'Good Lord. Has it been that long since last we spoke?'

Watson gave a tense shrug, and pulled a cigarette case from his pocket. 'It's been nearly five months. Other than the letter you sent from New York in July, the first word I've had from you in a great long time was your telegram this morning.'

Holmes drew in a little hiss of contrition between his teeth. 'I've never truly embraced the art of correspondence, have I?'

'Is that it? All this time I believed you still hadn't forgiven me for getting married.'

For a long moment the only sound in the room was the tick of the mantel-clock. Then Holmes turned away, unable to look his friend in the eye.

'It would be presumptuous of me to forgive,' he said, 'when I should be begging forgiveness.' Yet, truly remorseful as he was, now he found himself face to face with the parcel again he was unable to resist its lure. He reached out, touched the filthy string wrapped around it. 'I mean, to refuse to offer congratulations, or even to stand with you -' He rubbed the residue between forefinger and thumb. 'That. That was just -' Oily, a bit of grit. He should look at it under the microscope.

'You were afraid,' Watson said.

'What?'

'You were *afraid*, Holmes. Afraid that left to your own devices, your resolve would fail you. You feared you might lose your way again if I weren't there to keep you on the straight and narrow.'

'Not much of an excuse. But you see, we've come around full circle since those dark days, Watson. Come. Come look at the name on the package.' Watson didn't move, stubbornly resolved not to be intrigued. Holmes blew out a noisy sigh, and brought the filthy parcel to *him*, pointing at the faded brown scrawl. *G. R. Petra*.

'Oh, Dear Lord,' Watson whispered. 'Please tell me this package does not contain bones, hair, or body-parts.'

'Nothing so obvious. Much more mysterious. If I am correct, in this parcel I will find a pair of my own boots, which I consigned to the rubbish-heap some nine years ago.'

'Boots? Why would she…? God in Heaven. Not those damned boots again!'

LANCE PARKIN

AHISTORY

with additional material by

LARS PEARSON

AN UNAUTHORIS[ED]
HISTORY OF TH[E]
DOCTOR WH[O]
UNIVERS[E]

OUT NOW... Out of print for eight years, Lance Parkin's widely praised *Doctor Who* chronology, *A History of the Universe*, now returns as an updated volume - named *AHistory* - from Mad Norwegian Press.

Laying out the *Doctor Who* universe into a mindbendingly detailed timeline, *History* starts with the Big Bang and moves forward through the universe's development, tracing such keystone events as the imprisonment of the world-destroye[r] Sutekh, the rise and fall of the Earth Empire and much, much more. All in all, *Aistory* creates a chronicle of the universe's events in a manner befitting the Time Lords themselves.

The previous version of *History* (due to its publication date) didn't even include all o[f] the Virgin New Adventures, but Parki[n] here—exhaustively—expands *AHistory* t[o] take in the remainder of the Virgin novels, the Big Finish audios, the Telos novellas and every BBC *Doctor Who* novel up through his own *The Gallifrey Chronicles*, the conclusion of the Eighth Doctor nove[l] range.

MSRP: $24.95

www.madnorwegian.com

1150 46th St
Des Moines, IA
info@madnorwegian.com

**mad
norwegian
press**

POLICE PUBLIC CALL BOX

OPEN THE DOOR TO
A NEW DIMENSION

ww.galaxy4.co.uk

CREDITS

Publisher / Editor
Lars Pearson

Copy Editor
Steve Manfred

Interior/Cover Design
Christa Dickson

Associate Editors
Marc Eby
Dave Gartner
Joshua Wilson

Technical Support
Anthony Clifton

Publisher "Thank Yous" to...
Lance Parkin
Bill Albert
Jeremy Bement
Shawne Kleckner
Shaun Lyon
Robert Smith?
The Universal Network
of Iowan Time Lords

1150 46th Street
Des Moines, Iowa 50311
info@madnorwegian.com
www.madnorwegian.com